2MUCH4U

SCHOLASTIC

AUCKLAND SYDNEY NEW YORK LONDON TORONTO
MEXICO CITY NEW DELHI HONG KONG

To Ande for her
patience and support

Published by Scholastic New Zealand Limited, 1999
Private Bag 94407, Greenmount, Auckland 1730, New Zealand.

Scholastic Australia Pty Limited
PO Box 579, Gosford, NSW 2250, Australia.

Scholastic Inc
555 Broadway, New York, NY 10012-3999, USA.

Scholastic Limited
1-19 New Oxford Street, London, WC1A INU, England.

Scholastic Canada Limited
175 Hillmount Rd, Markham Ontario L6C 1Z7, Canada.

Scholastic Mexico
Bretana 99, Col. Zacahuitzco, 03550, Mexico D.F., Mexico.

Scholastic India Pte Limited
29 Udyog Vihar, Phase-1, Gurgaon-122 016, Haryana, India.

Scholastic Hong Kong
Room 601-2, Tung Shun Hing Commercial Centre,
20-22 Granville Road, Kowloon, Hong Kong.

ISBN 1-86943-416-1

9 8 7 6 5 4 3 2 0 1 2 3/0

Edited by Frances Chan
Cover artwork and illustrations by Fraser Williamson
Typeset in 11/15 pt Rotis Serif by Egan-Reid Ltd
Printed by SRM Production Services, Malaysia

Acknowledgements

Thanks to Whitirea Polytechnic for the opportunity to complete this book while enrolled in their Writing Course. Thanks also to the NZ Children's Book Foundation for the Tom Fitzgibbon Award.

Contents

1
Where it all Goes Wrong

Mum was going to give us a ride into town to see *Revenge of the Rotting Corpses* at the Carterton movie theatre. Normally we wouldn't have been allowed in because it was an R16, but Mrs Hamble, the ticket lady, had lost her glasses and when she had asked Tu what the rating was he said 'G'. Everyone was going: Vinny, Tu and Tammy the Terrible Tawhiti Twins, Connor McDonald – even my brother Matt, and he's way over 16.

The trouble was that Mum was still under the tractor. "We can't go anywhere till I've got this tyre off, burnt the rubbish, washed the car and made a salad to take to Pam's. You two can stand there looking like your throats have been cut or you can give me a hand."

Mum's really very nice when you get to know her, she's just a bit rougher than your average Mum.

We went up to the house and got things organised. I put a pot of eggs on the stove for a lettuce salad while Vinny took the rubbish down the hill a bit to the incinerator. Then I went to clean the car, it really needed it, you could hardly see the 'Clean Me' sign that Matt had rubbed into the dust a month ago. I pulled the hose out, but it wasn't quite long enough to reach to the front of the car.

I was ninety-nine percent sure that I wasn't allowed to shift the car, but since Mum was busy and I was doing her a favour I took the chance, unlocked the car, let the handbrake off and pushed it back a little with my foot. The car rolled gently back and stopped on a stone. I looked around to see if Vinny saw that fantastic piece of driving, but he was too busy burning something. I did see Rambo, our pet cow, come barging through the gate that Vinny had left open.

"The cow's getting in!" I yelled to Vinny as I leapt out of the car, slammed the door and sprinted to head her off. I'm nearly the fastest kid in our class but I was no match for Rambo as she galloped across our lawn to the vegie patch.

I stopped and turned to Vinny, "Come and give us a hand." Vinny shrugged and trotted up the hill. He stared at Rambo when he got there, she was munching happily on a salad of lettuce and silver beet. Vinny moved from the city about a year ago and he wasn't too sure about stock. Rambo took a step forward. Vinny backed towards the house.

"She's not going to charge, is she?"

"Course not," I said as I skirted around the lawn, Vinny followed. He made sure that I was always in a direct line between him and the cow.

"Man, what if she charges – do you run or lie on the ground and play dead?"

"She's not going to charge. She's our house cow, kind of like a pet. Stay there and make sure she doesn't go back around the house."

Vinny stood still and started waving his arms like he was doing aerobics. He's about my height but he's really skinny with dark hair and a huge nose. He looked like one of those puppets on a string. I went through what was left of the garden and started to sneak up behind the cow.

Meanwhile Mum was coming back from the shed rolling the tractor tyre in front of her. "What's going on here?" she called. She leant the tyre over on the car and started to stride towards us. I froze as the car started to move. The weight of the tyre pushed it over the stone and it started to gently roll down the drive.

"Nnnnnghhhhaaaar!" I screamed and ran towards it.

Rambo was directly between me and the car. She had never seen panic before. She thought she was going to be eaten raw. She ran for Vinny. Vinny dived to the ground and covered his head, Rambo ran back out the gate. Mum saw me running, then she saw the car. She made a flying tackle and pinned me to the ground. "You'll get run over," she gasped.

The car gradually picked up momentum. It left the drive and rolled down the grassy slope, picking up speed as it headed for the river at the bottom. "Awwwww no," I groaned, but I hadn't seen the incinerator. The car belted into the half-full drum; it crumpled and bounced ahead. The car caught it up and it wedged under the front bumper. Huge chunks of grass tore out as the car groaned and bounced to a halt on top of the drum.

"Thank God," whispered Mum. I let out a huge sigh.

"Aaaarrrrggh!" squawked Vinny. Smoke was wisping from underneath the car. The smoke got darker. Flames were creeping out of the bonnet and back towards the windscreen.

Gradually they spread, and smoke belched out from the body of the car and the paint turned black.

I turned to Mum, horrified. She watched for another moment then looked across at me, her face was crumpled, like she was going to cry. "My car . . ." she whimpered.

Vinny came and stood next to us. There was nothing we could do so we just stared. The flames had spread to the back of the car by now and they licked around the petrol tank. It blew up with a whooshing sound; a ball of orange flame erupted underneath the car and completely engulfed it.

"Faaaaa!" said Vinny and I together. Mum just shook her head.

"How could I have left the brake off?" she muttered to herself.

I felt my stomach tighten up. I'd raced to get the cow without putting the handbrake on, this was all my fault. "M . . . Mum, I gotta tell you something."

"It'll have to wait," she said as the neighbours pulled up in their ute to see what all the smoke was about.

I stood there feeling like I was going to throw up. I'd burnt our car out, it was completely ruined and it was all my fault. That was all that I could think; it was like a nightmare, too bad to even tell Vinny.

Eventually the fire brigade made it, but there wasn't much of the car left by then. All the tyres had burnt out, the windows melted and the interior burned out. They hosed down the wreck but there didn't seem much point.

Mum had had about enough of answering the neighbours' questions and went back up to the house. As soon as she opened the door a great black cloud of smoke came pouring out.

"Fire!" yelled Vinny.

The fire chief, Hank Hoser, had his back to the house.

"Of course it's a bloody fire," he said, but when he saw the rest of the brigade tearing up the hill with hoses and axes he turned around, saw the smoke and started yelling at the running men. "Get that unit up here! Break the windows! Get the axes!"

Vinny was first to the house. He realised exactly where the smoke was coming from so he waved at the firemen. I couldn't move, I just stood there watching.

"No, it's okay. Stop!" cried Vinny. They took about as much notice of him as I take of the morning notices at school.

"If any one of you steps inside my house in those filthy boots or even scratches the paint with an axe I'll have your guts for garters!" Mum yelled. The firemen stopped dead. She was standing in the doorway with a smoking saucepan in her hand. "Some eggs have boiled dry and blown up in there." She stared very hard at me. "There isn't a fire, but if you stay here for a bit I'm sure I can find a few cold beers."

There was a cheer from the firefighters and they quite happily waited for Mum. While they were sitting around drinking I heard Mum talking to Hank Hoser. "I can't understand it," she said. "I always leave the handbrake on. It's second nature to me."

"It's okay Antoinette," he said patting her on the arm. "These thing happen you know. It's just an unfortunate mistake."

2
Where it Gets Worse

"Faaaaa!" said Tu and Tammy together. We were on the bus and I'd just told them about the fire. I hadn't told them that I'd left the handbrake off.

"D . . . D . . . Did it blow up, l . . . l . . . like they do on TV?" asked Connor McDonald, leaning over the seats so that his red head was between the Tawhiti twins.

"Yeah," said Vinny, "it went up in a huge fireball. If we'd have been anywhere near it we would have been roasted alive. It was like a bomb going off."

"Faaaaa!" said Tu and Tammy again. They often talked at the same time and they looked nearly the same too, except that Tammy had longer hair and she was bigger than Tu.

"W . . . w . . . what did your Mum say about the c . . . c . . . cow?" asked Connor.

"And the eggs?"

I shrugged, hoping the subject would change, "Not much really."

"She couldn't say much," said Vinny. "She was the one that left the hand brake off."

I sank further into my seat, trying to hide. I felt like the coyote in the *Road Runner* cartoon, always making a mess of things. I just wished that I could fall off a cliff and into a hole, that way it wouldn't matter.

"What was *Revenge of the Rotting Corpses* like?" asked Vinny. "Was there heaps of blood and guts and sex and violence?"

"Nah," Tu screwed up his face. "Should've gone to your place and watched the car blow up."

"M . . . M . . . Mrs H . . . Hamble found her glasses just before the movie."

"Reckoned she couldn't show an R16 so she changed the film," said Tammy.

"What to?" asked Vinny.

"The *F . . . F . . . Famous F . . . F . . . Five Go F . . . F . . . F . . . Fishing*," stuttered Connor. Vinny and I groaned.

"We had to stay for the whole movie because Mum was picking us up. If she'd seen us on the streets she'd have killed us," frowned Tammy.

"Slowly," added Tu.

"Man," Vinny put on his most serious face, "you guys have all the fun. I wish I could have seen the Famous Five instead of Smith's Sizzling Subaru."

Tu hit him for being smart.

"Owww, that hurt."

"Lucky I didn't punch ya first," said Tammy. "Woulda been a lot harder than that." I agreed. Connor might be the tallest kid at school, but Tammy's the toughest.

School was a real drag that day, I couldn't think of anything but the car. Mr Hottom (we call him Bottom) our form teacher, was talking about conservation. I was thinking that if I took my helmet off and rode into a power pole really fast

I might get amnesia and forget that I wrecked our car.

"Davin Smith," Bottom said. "Don't you think that's a good idea?"

"Um, ah . . ." I looked at Vinny for help. He shrugged; he'd been tying a knot in his leather bracelet. I took a chance. "Absolutely not B . . . Mr Hottom. I don't think that's a good idea at all." The classroom was completely silent for the first time that day.

Mr Hottom raised his eyebrows, "Davin doesn't think that we should protect our endangered species. Why's that Davin?"

"I . . . ummm." I didn't know what to say. I could imagine everyone thinking that as well as wrecking my home I went around shooting kiwis and chainsawing native bush. "I wasn't listening to your question Mr Hottom. I think that we should protect our endangered species."

"That's right Davin, and I think that you should have lunchtime detention for not listening in class." I shrugged, I didn't really care.

Detention was alright, it meant I didn't have to answer everybody's questions about the fire. Vinny must have talked about it through most of lunchtime because nobody wanted to know anything during swimming or on the bus on the way home. That suited me fine.

I'd made up my mind that I was going to tell Mum about moving the car. I was ready to face the consequences rather than have this guilt hanging over me. Grounding for a year, no pocket money for life, bread and water. I'd done the crime I'd do my time.

The men from the tyre shop were at home when I got back, and a new tyre was on the tractor. "Thanks," said Mum as they were leaving, "I really need this old tractor now."

We watched their truck drive up the road. "Are you going to make some hay?" I asked.

"No."

"Then why do you need the tractor so much?"

"To get to town."

I stared at the old tractor. Mum had bought it off a guy who had used it for taking his boat to the boat ramp. The salty water had covered it in a deep red rust, except for the areas that were crusted in gobs of dried mud from our farm. The engine leaked oil and the seat had great tears in it where the stuffing was hanging out.

"You can't take that to town," I said.

Mum folded her arms across her chest. "What else am I going to take?"

I shrugged. "Aren't we going to get another car from the insurance?" I knew we had insurance, Mum had given me an envelope to post to them.

Mum pulled an envelope from her pocket. "Insurance companies don't pay out if you don't pay them. You forgot to post the cheque." I stared at the envelope, it looked like the same one that she'd given me two weeks before. I couldn't believe it, now we couldn't even get another car. I hung my head so Mum couldn't see my face.

"Where was it Mum?"

"Under your bed with your comics." I remembered now, I'd picked up some of Connor's comics the same day I was supposed to post the letter. I hadn't read them yet, the letter must have got mixed up with them.

I had to tell Mum about the car. "Mum . . ."

"Look Davin, I just don't want to hear another excuse, I've had it up to here with your excuses. You're always being careless and messing things up. When are you going to learn?"

"But Mum . . ."

"No Davin, I'm going to town now. Matt'll be here shortly. Just have a long hard think about what you've done." Mum strode off toward the house.

It was the end of the world. I stood there and waited for the sky to fall in or an earthquake to swallow me up. I could feel the tears coming. I went and sat on the woolshed landing and yeah, I blubbed for a while. It felt pretty awful but I think I felt better after I'd finished. That's what it was like for me anyway.

Mum came out of the house after a while with her town clothes on. I tried not to look at her but I could see her out of the corner of my eye. Her hair had been grey for as long as I could remember and her face was tanned and lined, making her look a lot older than forty. She's still slim though and she likes to get dressed up when she goes to town. She had this colourful summer dress on and a straw hat and her handbag.

I could hear Matt's motorbike coming and I guess Mum could too because she put her handbag on the tray of the tractor and climbed on. She started up the tractor. She must have been pretty upset because she took off up the drive in a real hurry. She didn't even stop to talk to Matt, in fact she nearly ran his motorbike off the drive. I suppose it would have looked pretty funny, Mum flying up the road on a tractor, hanging onto her hat in one hand and trying to steer and hold her dress with the other, dust billowing out behind her. Normally I would have laughed, but I couldn't even raise a smile.

3
Confession of an Arsonist

Matt pulled up on his motorbike and took his helmet off. He doesn't belong to a gang. He wears leathers, but that's so that if he falls off he won't get pasted all over the road. He's got really, really short hair and an earing in his left ear. He's okay for a brother except that he's always fighting with Mum.

"How are ya?" he grinned.

"Sod off," I said.

"Nice to see ya too. Sounds like it's all been

happening up here. I heard they were going to cordon this place off and declare it a national disaster area."

"What part of 'sod off' don't you understand?" I glared at him.

"Suit yourself." Matt shrugged and rode over to the house. He's a shearer and when he's not staying out at farms he lives in a caravan at the back of our place.

Vinny came over not long afterwards. He lives with his mother just down the road. She's got a lifestyle block and she wears really wild clothes and always gives Vinny these amazing vegetarian dishes for school lunch. I usually swap them for my cheese and Marmite sandwiches. He didn't see me, so I opened the door of the woolshed really quietly and slipped in. I knew my eyes were still red and I didn't want him to know I'd been crying.

It was cool and dark in there, and smelled of sheep. I lay down in a pile of wool and looked at the rafters. I used to come over here all the time when Dad was alive, play around the shed or watch him shearing. He was really strong and he could shear for hours at a time without even looking tired. He taught Matt to shear and I used to love sweeping up the wool with the radio on really loud and Dad singing along to it.

He'd make it look so easy while Matt'd be sweating and swearing and having a hard time. He was going to teach me to shear too. I really missed him.

I could hear the radio on over at the caravan, and someone laughing. I opened the door a crack and looked out. Matt and Vinny were sitting out in the sun in deck chairs. I still felt pretty miserable but I couldn't hide out forever. I washed my face in the sink and walked over to them.

"What's up with misery guts?" Matt nodded towards me as I walked up.

"I think he had a thing for that car." Vinny was wearing these new sunglasses that wrapped right around his head.

"Really?"

"Yeah it's pretty kinky but I think he was in love with it. He's heartbroken and has vowed never to ride in another car for as long as he lives."

"It could make headlines," said Matt. "Teenage Boy and Automobile in Love Triangle."

"Okay, but you need three for a triangle," laughed Vinny.

"It's that tractor – I always knew she was evil, she's trying to move in on him."

"Oh my God!" cried Vinny. "It was her all along, it was her tyre that pushed the car to her tragic death, unbelievable."

They started laughing, it was so sick that I couldn't help the tiniest grin.

"It smiles," said Matt.

"Cut it out you guys, you're really sick."

"We'll take that as a compliment, won't we Vinny? Grab a soft drink out of the fridge if you like, Dav." Matt nodded at the caravan. I got a can and sat down with them.

"So what's eating you?" asked Matt, who probably thought he was being subtle.

I shook my head, "Nah. I can't tell you, it's too much."

"Too much to tell your best mate and your brother?" asked Vinny.

"Murder, drugs, drunken orgies?" suggested Matt.

"No, I think it's his Mafia connections."

"Come on, this is serious," I said.

"More serious than all of that?" Matt thought for a moment. "You're in trouble with The Swampwitch aren't you?" The Swampwitch isn't some dreadful creature that lives in the mud and comes out to feed on sheep carcasses and innocent children, it's what Matt calls Mum.

I didn't say anything.

"That's definitely it. Have you been using her hair dryer again?" asked Vinny.

I glared at him.

"Is it about Dad?" asked Matt, really quietly.

I shook my head. They sat and looked at me, saying nothing, they just stared. Vinny squinted his eyes, Matt drummed his fingers on his knee.

"Come on you guys," I said, "it's private."

Matt kept on staring, humming a tune under his breath. Vinny sat like a rock. I couldn't stand this kind of torture.

"It's personal."

They didn't stop. It was driving me crazy.

"Alright I'll tell you," I said, "but not a word to anyone." They both nodded.

"Whew," said Matt when I finished. He disappeared into the caravan.

"Unbelievable," muttered Vinny.

Matt returned with two cans of beer. "I think we'd all better have a beer after that, or I'll have one, you two can share the other one."

Vinny and I passed our can back and forwards. The beer tasted pretty bad but we drank it anyway.

"I feel bloody awful," I said. "Mum can't afford this, she's going to have to drive that poxy old tractor everywhere. I haven't even told her it was me. I gotta pay her back somehow. What do I do?"

"You could leave town," suggested Vinny, "or the country, flee to Europe and start a wrecking business."

Matt frowned. "Come on Vinny, get real, this is some serious shit we're in." Sometimes I could just about hug him. "As I see it you've got two options – you could tell Mum and face the consequences."

"Second option?" I asked.

"Second option, you could not tell her."

"I couldn't just not tell her."

"Well tell her then," said Matt.

"I couldn't do that."

"I can see another option," said Vinny. "You could work over summer, earn lots of money for another car and tell her just before you give her the money."

Matt nodded. "It'd soften the blow a bit."

"And you wouldn't have to tell her for a while," said Vinny.

I thought about it, at least I'd be able to pay her back something. "What could I do?"

"Lots of things," said Matt. "Feeding animals, pulling ragwort, grubbing thistles, mowing lawns."

"Mum's got a whole stack of jobs that she wants me to do, I could charge her for them," I said.

"No way," Matt shook his head. "That'd be robbing Peter to pay Paul."

"What jobs have other people got then?" I asked.

"You could go babysitting or do all my jobs," said Vinny.

"No way!"

"Fair enough," Matt agreed. "But what does that idea sound like?"

"Hell," I said, "but it's better than riding into a power pole and getting amnesia."

"Lets drink to that," said Matt. He raised his can, Vinny and I both gripped ours and clunked it against his one. The beer was warm, flat and horrible but it felt a lot better to have told someone and to have a plan.

We hid the beer cans when we saw Mum coming back up the drive on the tractor. This time the whole tray was loaded up with groceries and shopping.

“Come on you lot, give us a hand with all this,” she called when she stopped the tractor.

“The Swampwitch beckons,” murmured Matt as we walked around to give her a hand. Matt and Vinny grabbed a handful of bags each.

“Give us a hand here would you Davin?” Mum was holding one end of a pile of wool packs. I reached over and grabbed the other end and we trundled over to the woolshed. We climbed the landing and put the packs in the door. I was about to walk out but Mum stayed where she was. “Davin?”

“Yeah Mum?”

She was fiddling with a piece of wool that she’d picked up, winding it around her fingers and back again. She looked up. “I’m sorry about all that before, about going on at you . . .”

“That’s alright ,” I said, embarrassed.

“No it’s not, it’s only that I was upset.”

“Mum . . .” I began.

“Hang on Davin, it’s just that your father was the same. I mean he was funny and gentle and kind, but he was careless and forgetful too.” Mum’s eyes were shiny, she looked right at me. “I think that’s how he had the accident and rolled the four wheeler, just a silly careless moment. That killed him Davin. I just couldn't stand it if something happened to you too. Just from a silly moment like that." Mum's voice got really shaky and she looked upset.

I was only going to give her a quick hug but she hung on so hard that it turned into a long one. Eventually she let go. "You're alright Davin, you know that?" she said. I was tempted to tell her about the car then but I didn't. I was determined to pay her back.

4
Teamwork

"Davin's working for the summer," announced Vinny on the bus. He was wearing a new tie-dyed shirt and baggy pants.

"Serious?" asked Tu.

"Yup," said Vinny. "He's going into business." I hardly ever get to answer my own questions if Vinny's there. He'd probably open my mail too except that I never get any.

"W . . . w . . . what sort of w . . . w . . . work?" asked Connor.

"Casual," I said quickly, before Vinny butted in.

Tammy frowned. "If you're going to be working don't you think that you should be serious about it? If they're paying you they'd probably want you to take it quite serious."

"Duuuuu," said Tu. "He means odd jobs and chores, not that 'casual'."

"Don't duuuuu me," Tammy thumped him.

"H . . . H . . . How are you going to l . . . l . . . let people know that you're looking for w . . . w . . . work?" asked Connor.

I looked at Vinny, he shrugged.

"I c . . . I c . . . I could do a flyer on the c . . . c . . . computer if you w . . . "

"Yeah," Vinny beat me yet again. "That's a great idea. We could put all the things that Dav can do and his phone number."

"I'll do some artwork on it," offered Tu.

"And we can drop them in everyone's letterboxes in the district," said Tammy.

"Wow," said Vinny in awe. "That's organised."

Everyone sat in silence for a while.

"Hey when's your cousin coming, Tammy?" asked Vinny.

"Next week, and she's going to stay all holidays."

"Awesome. It'll be a choice holiday." said Tu.

"Swimming in the creek," said Tammy.

"E . . . eeling," stuttered Connor.

"Sunbathing."

"Movies."

"Horse riding."

"M . . . m . . . motorbike riding."

I slumped in my seat and crossed my arms. "Working," I muttered.

"It's alright mate," said Vinny. "We'll visit you when we're sick of having fun."

"And think of all the money you'll have by the end of the summer," said Tu.

I rolled my eyes. "Think of all the money Mum'll have," I whispered to Vinny.

We were into our last week of school by now and things were pretty relaxed, even Bottom was nearly human. I suppose it's because he doesn't have to help organise a big concert like they do at other schools. We have our concert at the end of the second term. On the last day of school we have a big barbecue/sports day/party. Everyone stays up really late. Last year it was daylight before some of the parents got home.

Anyway, we designed my flyers at playtime, and everyone thought they were pretty good so we were dying to type them up on the computer. It was a fine day and we weren't supposed to be inside at lunchtime, but Bottom was in his office. We all trooped inside and Connor typed up the letter. He might not talk that quickly but he was a whiz on typing.

Amelia Bain, the class know-all was being a pain. "You're not supposed to be on the computers," she squealed.

"I'll sort her out," growled Tammy, moving towards her. We managed to stop her before she got to Amelia (it would have been hard to explain a missing kid and blood stains on the carpet), but Amelia must have been able to read minds. She started screaming and ran straight to Bottom's office.

Bottom came storming out. We all stepped back and looked guilty except for Connor, who was typing so fast he didn't even notice. Bottom walked up behind him and looked over his shoulder.

"Designing pamphlets, are we?" his eyebrows went up. Connor got such a fright that he swore. Bottom pretended not to notice.

"Yeah," I said, "we are."

"Very enterprising. Makes a change from playing computer games, doesn't it Vinny?" He was always catching Vinny out.

"It does," said Vinny. "Not nearly as much fun though."

"Hmmmm!" said Bottom and walked out again. Amelia was in the doorway waiting to see us get caught. When Bottom walked past she pouted.

"Don't be such a tell-tale," said Bottom on the way past.

"Unbelievable!" said Vinny.

"Faaaaa," agreed the Tawhiti twins together.

By the time Tu and Connor had finished the flyers they were pretty impressive. Vinny held one up and started reading it.

"2MUCH4U JOB SERVICE.
TOO MUCH TO DO THIS SUMMER? CALL 2MUCH4U
FOR ALL YOUR HOME AND FARM JOBS: FEEDING
ANIMALS, GRUBBING THISTLES, MOWING LAWNS,
TRIMMING HEDGES, DIGGING GARDENS.
YOU NAME IT WE'LL DO IT.
CONTACT DAVIN SMITH, (07) 827 7112.
PS. NO BABYSITTING."

Tu had drawn a picture of me (you could tell because I've got skinny legs, spiky hair and these ears that stick way out) running somewhere with a lawn mower, spade, hedge trimmer, and bag of dog biscuits in my arms and a spray knapsack on my shoulders. There were rakes, trowels and thistle grubbers flying out behind me.

"Choice," said Tammy, "but don't you think all that stuff flying out the back will give people the wrong impression?"

"Why?" asked Vinny. "He's always dropping and losing stuff, he's a walking disaster area."

"Y . . . yeah we know that," said Connor, "b . . . but the people he's working for won't."

"They'll find out pretty quick," laughed Vinny.

I ignored him. "I think it's a great picture Tu, thanks for doing it."

"No worries mate," he grinned. "Pretty cool name I reckon."

"2MUCH4U," said Tammy. "You could use that for a personalised plate."

"Put it on your tractor, aye Dav?" said Vinny. I glared at him. He's a great mate to have but I sometimes wish he wasn't such a smart-arse.

We decided that it'd be best to put the flyers out after the holidays had started. That way I could answer all of the thousands of phone calls and get to work on the jobs straight away. That gave me nearly a week of freedom before I started my working life. Well, not really, I still had to break the news to Mum.

I was going to tell her at teatime. I'd psyched myself into it, I'd even helped to peel the spuds. "Mum?" I asked as we sat down to cold mutton, salad and potatoes, "I want to ask you something."

Just then there was the sound of a car skidding on gravel. The front door slammed and someone was walking up the hall. "Matt," I suggested. He was the only one who would come straight in without knocking.

He walked into the kitchen in his greasy shearing clothes. "Hiya, what's for tea?"

"Nothing, " said Mum.

Matt looked at my plate. "Nothing with spuds and salad."

"Nothing," repeated Mum, "because you didn't tell me you'd be home for tea."

Matt frowned. "We finished our job, I thought I'd come back and surprise you."

"You thought you'd come back for a free dinner."

Mum picked up the pepper mill and ground pepper furiously.

"Where's your motorbike?" I asked, trying to break the tension.

"In town," Matt said.

"Too drunk to ride home?" asked Mum, banging the pepper shaker on the table.

"Yeah," said Matt, "thought you'd be pleased I didn't ride it."

"I'd be more pleased if you hadn't been at the pub," said Mum. They weren't exactly yelling at each other but Mum and Matt always seem to get in these sort of discussions. I hated to see them fight.

"So I can't have any tea?" asked Matt, standing with his arms crossed.

"Not until you've cleaned yourself up," Mum didn't look at him. Matt made a face to me and walked out the door.

"Davin, now what did you want to talk about before we were so rudely interrupted?"

"Um, I can't remember," I lied. She glanced up at me quickly.

"Davin Smith don't lie to me. I'm not some ogre even if your brother thinks I am."

I was caught now. "I . . . I'm keen to do some work over summer."

"Great, I've got lots for you to do."

"No," I said. "Paid work around the district, mowing lawns and digging gardens and things. Here, I'll show you." I ran to my room and got Mum the flyer. "I was going to get it photocopied and the guys would help me put it in letterboxes around the district."

"Mmmm," said Mum, reading. "2MUCH4U . . . very good." She looked at the flyer for a moment then looked up and smiled. "I think that's a great idea, keep you out of trouble for a while. Good on you for showing some initiative."

"Thanks Mum," I said, amazed. It looked like 2MUCH4U was going to get off the ground.

5
Desiree Davidson

I didn't want to ride into the end-of-year party on the back of the tractor.

"I don't want to go," I told Mum as she climbed into the driver's seat.

"You're going." Mum turned the key and the tractor slowly chugged into life, sending a cloud of black smoke into the air.

"This thing's an environmental hazard, we can't ride on it."

"Want me to tie you up and throw you on the back?"

"Aw Mum."

"Get on." She started to get out of her seat again.

"Swampwitch," I muttered as I stepped onto the tray and sat on the chilly bin.

Mum operated the hydraulics and the whole tray lifted off the ground. We chugged down the drive.

It wasn't too bad once we got on the main road. It was starting to feel like summer, and the wind rushing past my back was warm and smelt of hay. I sat watching the road behind me, hoping that no-one would come. I noticed that I could smell other things too. I smelt the pines first, then some silage, the piggeries along the road and some possums that hadn't made it across.

In the distance I saw the Tawhiti's van coming along behind us. I glanced around the tray but I already knew that there was nothing that I could hide behind, or under. They caught us up on a long straight; no-one was coming so Mr Tawhiti pulled right up next to us. Mr Tawhiti used to shear with Dad, he was a great big happy man. Mrs Tawhiti was a little wee thing, Tu and Tammy were both bigger than she was now. She leaned out the window. "Funny time to be getting the cows in, Ants," she joked. "Didn't you know there was a party on tonight?"

"Hell's bells," cried Mum, "a party? Why wasn't I told? Where is it? Who's going to be there?"

"Only men, rich, good-looking men. You'd better send this lot home on the tractor. We'll take the van in."

They carried on like this for about a minute. Tu and Tammy were in the back and I could see someone else in there too, sitting next to Tammy. She had a long, dark pony tail so I thought it must have been their cousin. Tu was laughing at me so I looked around, opened the chilly bin and pulled a beer can out. Tu said something and Tammy and her cousin turned around too. I saw the cousin for the first time. She was gorgeous. She had dark skin and a shy smile that made her look just like one of those supermodels. We hit a pothole and I nearly fell off the back of the tractor.

Tu was nodding his head and pointing at the can of beer and at himself. I reached out towards the van and he reached out of his window. There was still half a metre between us so I threw the can over, he passed it back to Tammy who was giggling and laughing with her cousin. Tu was motioning for me to throw over another one. I shook my head. Tu kept motioning, I shook my head, crossed my arms and sat on the chilly bin.

"Hey! We'll see you when we get there," called Mrs Tawhiti.

"Righto," Mum waved and the Tawhitis pulled ahead of us. Tu and Tammy waved, and the super model gave one of those shy smiles and waved too. I waved back, stood up and watched them drive away. I couldn't wait to catch up with them at school, especially their cousin.

"Sit down before you fall down," called Mum. I sat down. "And don't go giving all my beer away, I'll have nothing to drink." She looked back and winked at me.

Mum parked the tractor in the school paddock with all the other cars. Some of the younger kids pointed and laughed when they saw me on the back but I just ignored them, I was looking for the Tawhitis. I found Vinny first. "Mate," he said, "have you seen the Tawhiti's cousin, Desiree?"

"Yeah," I said trying to be cool and relaxed.

"Man, is she hot. I reckon I've got a chance there."

I suddenly lost my cool and relaxed look, I had competition.

"It's in the stars. This month they say 'Someone new brings romance into your life.' This has gotta be it."

"You don't really believe in that stuff do you?" I asked.

"I'm convinced, they're definitely onto something."
Things suddenly didn't look as bright. Vinny always had something to say and he had a whole wardrobe of trendy clothes. What sort of a chance did I have?
"Let's go and find everyone," I said.

Everyone was down on the field. Bottom was organising a game of touch rugby for anyone that wanted to play. We stood with Connor, Tu and Tammy and their cousin. "You fellas, this is Dessy. Dessy this is Connor and Vinny and Davin," said Tammy. We all said g'day and nodded uncomfortably. Up close Dessy was even nicer looking than in the van. She was quite tall and she had shorts on. They showed off an awesome pair of long, dark legs. Bottom came and sorted us into teams straight away.

"Right," he said, "Tu and Vinny and, who's this?"

"Dessy, my cousin," said Tu.

"Right Dessy," said Bottom, "you're all playing for The Hurricanes. Tammy, Connor and Davin are playing for The Crusaders. Let's go."

It took a few minutes for everyone to get to grips with playing touch. Connor dropped a pass early on, then Tu did the same thing.

Our team scored a touchdown in the left corner then The Hurricanes got the ball.

Vinny flicked a pass out to Dessy who ran towards Connor.

Tu was calling for the ball, "Outside you, feed the backs." Dessy looked like she was going to pass it, but she threw a dummy then straightened up. Connor was completely sucked in and Dessy ran for the line. I was closest so I sprinted to try and tag her before she scored. I would have caught her just before the line but she looked over her shoulder, saw me coming, threw the ball in the air and stopped. I had nowhere to go and I ran straight into her. We both ended up in a pile on the ground. Tammy, who was running along behind, caught the ball and charged straight past us to score.

"Aw shit, sorry," I said, trying to get off her without causing any more damage. I could feel my face going red, and it didn't help that Tu was standing there laughing his head off.

"Whew Davin aye, keep it to yourself."

Vinny joined in. "You've gotta watch him Dessy, he does this to all the girls."

Dessy was shaking. I thought that I'd hurt her, but when she got up she started laughing. "Y . . . you should have seen yourself try to stop, you looked so funny." I couldn't help smiling back, even though it was me that she was laughing at. It wasn't like she was teasing me, it just cracked her up.

The game was really close, but Vinny was trying to show off and held onto the ball too long. Tu got sick of it. "Don't be greedy man, the rest of us are playing too."

"Yeah," said Dessy, "you can pass it you know." Vinny went really quiet and I think he passed it every time after that.

Desiree was a pretty good touch player, faster than any of the other girls but she freaked out when someone was chasing her. She only dropped the ball once, when Tu gave her a bad pass. She just laughed and ran back into position. She was really cool about the whole thing.

Bottom called full-time after both teams had scored twice more; that made it a draw and everyone was happy. We all trooped up to the school lawn and helped ourselves to the barbecue tea that the parents had put on. I got mine and looked for somewhere to sit. There was a seat right next to Dessy but I was too embarrassed and sat further down, next to Tu. We ate for a minute then Tu elbowed me. "Watch Mr Smooth over there." He nodded towards the end of the seats. Vinny was just sitting down in the seat next to Dessy.

"G'day," he said, turning towards Dessy. "You play a really good game of touch, are you a Libra?" Tammy was also sitting next to Dessy. She was half-way through a mouthful and started giggling, food spraying back all over her plate.

"Gross," laughed Dessy, not knowing quite where to look.

Vinny tried again. "Desiree's a really neat name, I've never heard it before."

This time Tammy nearly fell off the seat laughing. Dessy turned towards Vinny but Tammy grabbed her arm. "You've got beautiful eyes," she said dramatically. "My God they're such a deep, mysterious brown." Dessy couldn't help it, she burst out laughing, so did Tammy, Tu and I. Vinny went bright red and sat on the end of the seat looking uncomfortable. As usual Connor came to the rescue.

"Hey V . . . V . . . Vinny," he said as he walked up with his dinner. "D . . . Did you get some v . . . v . . . venison?"

"No," said Vinny quietly.

"There's some on the barbie, M . . . M . . . Mum said to help yourself."

Connor didn't have to ask twice, Vinny was over at the barbie in a shot. Tammy started nudging Dessy after him. Dessy thumped her arm and scowled.

This time Vinny came back and sat with the rest of the guys. "Lucked out there," said Tu.

"Hmmm," mumbled Vinny.

"Bad luck mate," I said, quietly pleased. "Looks like the stars have got it wrong."

"It's early days, Dav, early days."

The rest of the night went pretty much as usual. The parents sat up drinking and talking while we tried pinching any half-finished drinks. Tammy and

Dessy were talking so the guys went down to the field and had a game of bull rush (it was a lot safer without Tammy Tawhiti playing).

Mum got me about midnight and we drove home on the tractor. She was in a good mood and I could hear her humming to herself as she drove. I felt good too, it was the start of the holidays and I was sure I was going to see some more of Desiree Davidson.

6
The Hounds of the Huntervilles

The 2MUCH4U flyers went out on the Friday that school finished. On Saturday morning I was prepared for a constant stream of phone calls. While I was brushing my teeth I was practising my phone answering technique.

"Guuuu murrring, 2Maaaaaffuuuuyuu," I said through a toothbrush and a mouthful of toothpaste. Mum came up behind me in her dressing gown.

"Try answering the phone like that and they'll think they've got a direct line to a Chinese takeaway."

"Vewwwy funnngy," I said and spat the toothpaste out. The phone rang in the hall, Mum started to move but I shot past her and picked it up.

"Good morning, 2MUCH4U job service, can I help you?"

"Sorry, wrong number," said Matt sounding confused on the other end of the line.

"No it's me," I said quickly.

"Who?"

"Davin."

"Oh right . . . I see, you've started up that job thing, good on ya," he said.

"I won't be starting anything up if you don't get off the phone and let the real customers on."

"Alright, keep your hair on. Put The Swampwitch on will ya."

"Mum it's for you." She came up the hall and took the phone. "Could you be quick please, I might have some customers calling," I said. Mum just raised her eyebrows.

I was getting a bowl of cereal when Mum came back into the kitchen. "Matt might be staying for a few days – he's going to ring back in a minute, when he knows if he's working or not."

"Great," I muttered. "More fights."

Mum frowned and went out to get changed. The phone rang. "Could you get that?" Mum called from her room.

"Righto." I picked up the receiver. "Yeah Matt, are you coming back for a day or two?"

"Pardon?" said a man's voice on the other end of the line. It definitely wasn't Matt.

"Aw . . . um, 2MANY4U jobs speaking," I was totally flustered, not the cool, suave businessman I wanted to be.

"You're the one who advertised for work?" He sounded uncertain.

"Yeah that's right."

"Okay, this is John Hunterville speaking. I've got to head away for a week, do you think you'd be able to feed my dogs?"

I knew Mr Hunterville lived about two kilometres up the road. "Yeah, I'm sure I can do that."

"That'd be great, listen, I've got to go this morning so I can't show you where everything is. There's a walk-in freezer just by our back porch . . ." He went on to tell me where everything was and what to do. "I'll leave a note at the back door in case you forget any of that. I'll pay you ten dollars a day, is that alright?"

"That'd be fine."

"Righto then." He paused for a moment. "Good luck with them." Then he hung up. The way he said it it sounded like I would be dealing with a pack of rabid hyenas rather than a few dogs. I should have taken it as a warning.

I stayed around home all morning, waiting for phone calls. Mum wasn't very helpful. She reckoned that since I was there I may as well be doing something useful so she made me do the vacuuming and the lawns. "I could be doing this for money," I protested.

"Do you want to keep your pocket money?" she growled.

"Yeah."

"Well do the jobs."

Vinny came around about three o'clock. He was wearing a new pair of trendy Nike sandals and a surfie top. I think his Mum must have shares in a surf shop. "Wanta go down the river?" he asked.

"Can't, I've gotta feed Mr Hunterville's dogs."

"S'pose you want me to come too," he grunted.

"Can if you like. I'm not splitting the pay though." He started raving on about the oppression of unemployed students by the capitalist majority. I ignored him and he came along.

The Hunterville's house was hidden from the road by trees. I'd never been there before. Vinny and I rode our bikes slowly up the drive. "It's quiet isn't it?" whispered Vinny.

"Yeah." It was deathly quiet among the trees. They were heavy with moss and damp, even though it was a hot day. A skinny stray cat slunk into the bushes in front of us. We could see glimpses of the house through the trees, but all we could make out was its bulk.

Suddenly we rounded a corner and it loomed in front of us, a huge old house with paint peeling off the walls and a section of gutter hanging from the roof. The lawns hadn't been mown, grass and shrubs grew right up to the old concrete steps.

"Wow, spooky," whispered Vinny.

"I'll say."

The drive ended in a loop at the front of the house

so we left our bikes there and walked down a trampled path that led to one side. We were just about at the corner when I heard a chain rattle. I stopped. "What was that?"

Vinny's eyes widened. "What?"

The chain rattled again. Suddenly a huge white shape leapt out from under the house in a growling, snarling frenzy. It lunged at Vinny.

"Aaaargh!" he cried as the pig dog hit the end of its chain and pulled up just millimetres from his leg. There was an explosion of sound from the back of the house, a chorus of barking, snarling dogs. Vinny flung himself at the fence and was in the paddock before I had a chance to move. "Save yourself!" screamed Vinny.

"It's chained up!" I yelled.

"Grrrrr," snarled the dog, its teeth bared and the hair standing up on its massive shoulders.

I kept out of its reach and went towards Vinny. He was staring at the dog.

"Sounds like there's a lot of them." I motioned to where the barking was coming from. Vinny just nodded. I edged forwards and looked around into the backyard. The pack were tied up to nearly every available object – to trees, under the house, around old car wrecks. There were a few sheep dogs, black and tan huntaways – but these were dwarfed by the pig dogs. There were at least fifteen of them and every one was massive. Big white and pink dogs with black markings, heavy striped animals with huge heads, stubby black dogs as wide across as they were tall. Many were covered in scars and scratches, some with fresh scabs across the top. All of them stood barking or growling, straining on their leashes.

"Shit!" I said. I didn't want to go further into the yard, my heart was already thumping and my hands felt shaky. I was terrified of the dogs, but what'd happen if they weren't fed? I could picture them killing and eating each other or gnawing through their chains and dragging women and children from their beds.

I had to do it. I turned to Vinny. "Are you coming?" He shook his head and backed further into the paddock. I sighed and advanced carefully into the yard, around one dog and past the snapping jaws of another. The freezer was where Mr Hunterville had said it was. It was a great refrigerated container with a heavy door on the front. I opened it and retreated into the cold. At least the dogs couldn't get me there.

Each day's food was in a big tray with the date labelled on it. I found the pile marked 'December 18'. It was a stack of goat meat, frozen ribs and legs sticking out with the skin still attached.

Mr Hunterville had said to feed them the meat frozen. There was no way I could lift the whole tray out so I grabbed two frozen legs and went into the yard. The pack went crazy when they saw the meat, throwing themselves the full length of their chains and falling back into the dust. "I hope those chains hold," I called to Vinny.

"I'll be at your funeral if they don't."

"Crap, you'll still be running." I threw the meat to the first two dogs I saw and they fell on it, gnawing and crunching at the frozen lumps. I gradually carted the pile outside. After I fed the closest ones I had to go past them to get to the others. I sneaked past them as they snarled and bristled, jaws full of goat meat.

Every time one moved I jumped back and my forehead was sweating even though my hands were frozen from the meat. I hoped the dogs couldn't smell how scared I was. Finally I only had one dog left to feed. My hands were numb but I managed to pick up the last lump of meat. I was edging past an angry looking black dog when I lost my grip on the meat and dropped it on the ground. I bent over to pick it up.

"Look out!" cried Vinny as the dog lunged at me. I jumped back, tripped on a pipe and fell backwards.

Suddenly a massive tiger-striped animal was by my head, saliva dripping from its jaws. It was the only dog that hadn't been fed.

"Run!" screamed Vinny. "Get outta there." The dog came at me. I screamed and pulled my arms over my head. I waited for the teeth to dig into me and rip chunks of meat out. Nothing happened.

I peeked through my arms and saw the dog had the piece of meat that I'd been carrying in its teeth and was growling and backing towards its kennel. I sat up slowly and inched away, keeping my eyes on the dog. It dropped the meat and moved towards me. I moved faster than I had ever moved, there was just a cloud of dust from the back yard to the side of the house.

"Faaaaa, that was close," said Vinny. "I thought you were a goner."

"Thanks for helping mate," I said sarcastically.

"Get off, you would have been torn to pieces by the time I got over there."

Vinny grinned. "Anyway, you're just earning your money."

I gave him the fingers and looked around at the dogs. They were quiet now, except for the sound of gnawing and crunching bones. Thankfully they all had water troughs and I didn't have to give them water as well. That would have been too much.

It was a relief to pick up our bikes and get out into the bright December sunshine. I stood on my pedals and biked flat out for a hundred metres. "I'm alive!" I yelled back at Vinny. "I'm alive!"

"For now, but you've gotta go back tomorrow and do it all again."

7
Rough Riding

Vinny said that he'd had enough excitement for one day so he carried on past our place and went home. When I got up to the house I saw Matt's motorbike. I should have known that he'd be arguing with Mum. I heard them as soon as I walked in the back door. "I told you you'd ruin your back," Mum was saying.

"It's just a bit sore Mum, it's not ruined." I walked into the kitchen. Mum was hacking up some onions at the bench, Matt was lying on the kitchen floor with a heat lamp on his back.

"A few more years of shearing and it will be," Mum said, weepy-eyed and sniffing from the onions.

"Hi Mum, hi Matt," I said, trying to sound cheerful.

"Mmmm," grunted Matt, shifting the lamp.

"You should show some initiative, like Davin here, go out and find a real job."

"I haven't got a real job Mum, I'm just doing casual work," I said.

"But you're showing initiative," said Mum, waving the knife at me," and your brother could learn something from that."

Matt looked up and rolled his eyes at me.

"And don't you be cheeky either Matt, you're too old for that sort of carry on."

"I'm too old to have my Mum telling me what to do too," said Matt.

"That's what you get when you're still living at home," growled Mum.

"Soon fix that," he muttered.

"Aye?" Mum sliced angrily into another onion.

"Soon fix that," he said, getting off the floor. "I'm looking for a flat in town."

"Hah!" Mum was in full cry now. I wished Matt wouldn't wind her up when she's like that, I hate seeing them arguing. "You'll soon find out what it's like flatting, no more going home and expecting a free meal. You wouldn't last a week."

The phone rang and I rushed into the hall to answer it. I could still hear them going at it in the background.

"Hello, 2MUCH4U job service, can I help you?"

"Yeah I think so mate, can you ride a horse?"

"Ummm, yeah." I'd ridden our pony when I was younger, I thought that'd count.

"Great, see I've got a horse up here that needs a bit of work. I'm laid up with a bust leg an' I can't do it. Whaddya reckon?"

"I s'pose," I said. "Who am I talking to?" I could hear Matt and Mum yelling in the background.

"Sorry mate, Murray Todd here, I'm the manager up at Kuratau Station." That was a few kilometres up the road, right next to the Tawhiti's place. I could just see myself galloping up to their place on a big black stallion.

"Yeah, that'd be great."

"Okay mate, come up here tomorrow afternoon and

we'll see how you go. If you're any good you can have the job for a month or so."

"Um, alright." He hung up and I walked back towards the kitchen. I heard the door slam just before I got there. Mum was standing in the middle of the room, her face was all red and she was staring at the door.

"You alright Mum?"

"Yes," she said sharply. I heard the motorbike start up and roar down the drive, it had obviously been a pretty big fight. I put the jug on to make Mum a strong cup of coffee.

"Do you know Murray Todd?" I asked.

"Cowboy Todd? Yeah, he used to win all the rodeos around here, manages Kuratau Station now." Mum stared out the window.

"He wants me to ride a horse for him while he's got a broken leg." I was expecting Mum to say that I couldn't do it because I couldn't ride very well but she didn't say anything, just stared out the window.

Mum and I were up watching TV till late. I heard Matt's bike pull in at about ten o'clock. He didn't come inside and Mum didn't even look up.

I biked up to Kuratau Station early the next

afternoon. The station looks over the Tawhiti's place. There were a couple of people at their house and I could see two figures on a horse in a nearby paddock.

There was a horse in one of the yards and I walked over to have a look. It tossed its head at me and whinnied, then it kicked up its heels and raced around the yard. It was a lot bigger than our pony and it definitely looked more frisky.

"That's the bugger," someone called from behind me. I looked around, a man was hobbling towards me on crutches. He had a wide brimmed hat pulled down over his eyes and wore one cowboy boot, the other foot was in plaster. "Murray Todd's the handle, you must be Davin." He stuck out his hand and shook mine so hard that it left a white mark when he let go. He had a tanned face with light blue eyes that twinkled, surrounded by wrinkles. I couldn't tell how old he was.

"Right," he said hobbling towards the yard. "Firebrand here's a little frisky. That's why I need someone to ride him, y'know, to settle him down. Nobody's been on him since he broke my leg."

"He broke your leg?" I asked nervously.

"Yeah, it was nothing really. I lost my grip while he was bucking, landed awkwardly. He gets a bit girthy, y'know."

This was sounding worse and worse. I had to get out of it. "Listen, I haven't actually done a lot of riding. I don't think this is such a good idea."

Cowboy Todd didn't seem to be on the same wave length. "Nah, you'll be right, just put one leg on each side and your mind in the middle, if you feel your mind slipping you'll know something's not right."

He went through the gate and picked a bridle off the rail. I followed him. "Get around behind him, be a bit careful though, he might kick. Then chase him up to me, there's a good lad."

"But . . . " I began.

"Quick, we haven't got all day." I sighed and did what he asked.

"Look Mr Todd." I started to explain, but he threw Firebrand's saddle on and I had to jump aside as the horse swung around.

"Just get round the other side and pass the girth under," called Cowboy. I passed the girth under without getting kicked. Firebrand shifted skittishly.

"Stand back," called Cowboy as soon as he had

the strap in his hand. He pulled it up and Firebrand swung around, kicking and rearing. Cowboy hung onto the reins until the horse finally calmed down.

My hands were sweaty now. There was no way I could ride this horse, I'd be thrown off and knocked unconscious. I thought for a moment, there was a chance I'd get amnesia, and I wouldn't have to tell Mum about the car.

"Right Davin, up ya get," said Cowboy.

I gritted my teeth and walked towards the horse. "This better be worth it," I muttered.

Cowboy gave me the reins. "Just remember, don't let your mind slip."

It already has, I thought.

As soon as I was in the saddle Firebrand reared up on his hind legs. I hung onto his mane, hoping that amnesia wasn't painful. Suddenly the horse came down and streaked around the yard.

"Yeeha," Mr Todd called, waving his hat. "What he wants is a bit of room."

"No!" I screamed, but he didn't take any notice, he had the gate open the next time we raced around the yard. Firebrand saw the gap and bolted through it. He stretched out faster and faster. I hauled back on the reins, but he lifted his head then threw it forward, ripping them out of my hand.

We flashed past the letterbox and out onto the road.

"Atta boy," cried Cowboy in the distance, "run it out of him."

Firebrand swerved into the Tawhiti's drive and bolted towards the paddock where I'd seen the horse. I pulled back on his mane but nothing happened. I could see Tammy and Desiree on a horse just inside the gate, staring at us. I was sure Firebrand wasn't going to stop and we were going to hit the gate. "Look out," I yelled. Tammy looked puzzled.

"Move!" I waved one hand in the air. To my surprise Firebrand stopped. I didn't. He dug his hooves into the drive and skidded to a halt. I sailed over his head and over the gate. Tammy had turned her horse around and its backside was facing me. I thought I was going to fly straight into it and have to be surgically removed. Instead I crash-landed in a swampy bit of ground behind the horse.

So much for galloping up on a black stallion. I carefully moved all my limbs, nothing was broken and I could still remember the car burning. It was a complete disaster.

I opened my eyes and stared straight up at the horse's arse.

"Looks like he's still alive," said Desiree, looking over her shoulder. I could see Tammy nodding.

"Kia ora Davin, can you hear me?" yelled Tammy.

"Course I can hear you," I mumbled.

"I don't think he's brain damaged," said Tammy to Dessy, "least not any more than usual."

I made a sour face and pulled myself out of the mud. Desiree climbed off from behind Tammy and went through the gate to where Firebrand was snorting and tossing the reins around.

"Take it easy," I called, "he's pretty wild." She nodded then held out her hand and approached the horse.

"Come on boy, you're a nice fella, come and see what I've got." I can't blame Firebrand for coming up to her, I would have done the same thing if I was in his position.

"Is Cowboy Todd getting you to ride his racehorse for him?" asked Tammy.

"Racehorse?" I turned towards her.

"Yeah, he's entering it in the Carterton Guineas."

"I'm not riding that horse anywhere." I looked over to Desiree who was swinging into the saddle.

"Don't, he'll kill you!" I squawked. Firebrand took a few prancing steps and she pulled in hard on the reins.

"Whoa boy, whoa." He went around in a tight circle, pulling at the bit but Desiree held him in.

"She's pretty good, aye?" said Tammy, grinning from ear to ear.

"Yeah," I breathed.

Firebrand jumped and pranced but Desiree kept a tight grip and talked to him all the time. Her eyes were sparkling by the time he settled down enough to stand still. "He's awesome," she cried. "Is he yours?"

I shook my head and pointed up the drive as Cowboy Todd was hobbling towards us. Firebrand pranced sideways and Desiree let him trot back towards the walking figure. She jumped down and talked to Cowboy for a minute then he led the horse away and she walked back. "Tumeke!" she yelled when she was within shouting distance. "He just offered me a job riding the horse."

"Too much!" called Tammy.

"Good on ya," I said, not knowing quite how I felt about that. The girls started chatting excitedly about the rides they could do. I listened for a while then limped towards Kuratau Station to get my bike and ride home again.

I fed Mr Hunterville's dogs on the way home. After Firebrand they seemed quite tame really. The same dog jumped out from under the house but I was ready for him. I picked a better route around the kennels too, so none of them came close to eating me.

8
Busting a Gut

When I got home there was a van outside Matt's caravan. I walked over and glanced into the back. Matt's gear was in it, his motorbike posters, the calfskins he'd cured, his weights. Matt walked out of the caravan with an armful of gear. "2MUCH4U, I've got a job for you," he said and winked.

"Yeah?"

"You can give us a hand moving out." I already knew he was going to say that. I just hadn't wanted to hear it from him.

"Where are you going?" I asked.

"To Sharon's place."

Sharon was one of the rousies in the shearing gang. "Are you sleeping with her?" I asked.

Matt kicked at me, but I moved and he missed. "No I'm not, I'm just flatting there, you've got a filthy mind."

"Wonder where I got that from?" I asked, looking at the posters of naked girls around the room.

"Smart-arse, I'm not paying you to look at the posters. Give me a hand."

"Paying," I slapped a hand to my forehead. "The only time you ever paid me was when I caught you nicking Mum's beer."

Matt put his armful down and folded his arms. "You want the money or not?"

"It's worth ten bucks an hour," I said.

"I'll give you seven."

"Eight."

"Seven fifty or the deal's off."

I scratched my chin, it was smooth compared to Matt's dark stubble. "Alright."

We got to work straightaway. It didn't take long really, Matt didn't have a lot of stuff.

"Right," said Matt, looking at the empty room, "I s'pose that's that."

"Want a hand unloading?"

"No thanks, I've gotta leave the van in town and you know you're not allowed on the motorbike with me."

Mum came over with a bacon and egg pie that she put in the front of the van. "That'll keep you fed tonight," she said.

"Ta," said Matt, walking towards the front of the van.

"You come here Matthew Smith," growled Mum.

"Aye, what'd I do now?"

Mum walked up to him, threw her arms around him and gave him a huge hug. She has these emotional outbursts occasionally. "You look after yourself," she said, letting him go, "and come around for tea next week."

"Okay Mum . . . thanks, I mean for everything." He shrugged and got into the van. We watched him drive away.

"Cunning bugger," I said as he disappeared.

"What?"

"He didn't pay me."

"Huh," said Mum. "Serve you right for charging him. You've got another job for tomorrow anyway. Mr Harnett rang up and he wants you to spray some ragwort."

I groaned. "That'll be fun."

"Hmm, he's okay I suppose but you keep away from his boys, they're trouble. They should be the ones spraying ragwort, not you."

"Hell no," I said. "Too much like hard work."

Old Mr Harnett looked like he'd been in a horrific accident. One leg stuck out to the side, he only had one arm, one eye and one ear. Well he had two ears, but only one worked. The good ear was on the opposite side to the good eye and when he talked to you he'd turn his head so that he could hear and squint past his broken nose with his good eye. Everyone called him Buzzard, including his sons who said it to his face.

I don't know if they ever had real names, everyone called them Oil and Scuz.

Oil had long dark greasy hair and a moustache. It was that greasy that when he used to go swimming (only when he was at school and the teacher could find him) he'd leave a shiny oil slick across the pool.

Matt reckoned that if it was refined and bottled they could put BP out of business.

Scuz on the other hand had very little hair, it was so short you could see his shiny white scalp underneath. He was a scrawny, weedy guy and he always wore black jeans and steel capped boots. He used to work as the presser in Matt's shearing gang but he'd kicked one of the sheep to death and Mr Tawhiti fired him. He'd threatened to kill Mr Tawhiti after that. They didn't seem to do any work on the farm, they just drove around in a big black Holden car.

I put on my overalls and gumboots and biked around to Harnetts at nine o'clock the next morning. The house was surrounded by old car bodies and farming equipment. Mr Harnett (Buzzard) came limping towards me through the cars. He limped really fast and with his bad eye I expected him to fall over. "You're the one then?" he squinted at me and rubbed his chin, he had no teeth so it seemed to stick out a long way.

"Yeah, you wanted some ragwort sprayed?" I asked.

"That's right, there's a bit around." I looked out across the farm. 'A bit' didn't really describe the amount of ragwort, it was everywhere. The only area without it was a watermelon patch by the road.

"What's your rate?" he asked, staring at me.

"Seven-fifty," I said.

"Seven-fifty," he repeated slowly. "Come on." He suddenly scuttled over to a pile of junk and came up with an old brass sprayer and an ancient looking flagon of spray. He gave me some rubber gloves and showed me how to mix the spray with water and how to use the sprayer. It was held together with bits of wire and gave off a thin dribble of spray when you pumped the handle really fast.

I started with a paddock by the drive. I walked down a strip pumping as fast as I could. There was red dye in the spray so that I could see where I'd been. Then I walked back. The tank was heavy and my shoulders and arms were sore before I even did an hour's work.

I kept having to fill the sprayer so I'd glance at my watch and work out how much money I'd earned. "Half an hour and that's $3.75 . . . an hour $7.50 . . . an hour and a half and that's $11.25." Bottom would have been amazed, I never even had a calculator to use.

The day got hotter and hotter. My overalls kept the spray off my skin but they were really hot and sticky. At eleven o'clock I saw the black Holden rolling into the driveway. I was close to the fence when it stopped alongside me, its engine still rumbling under the bonnet.

I tried to look in but couldn't see through the tinted windows. I carried on, trying not to look at the dark car sitting on the drive.

Suddenly the horn blared and I jumped. When I looked around Oil had his window down and was laughing and slapping the side of the car. "Haw, (thud) haw, (thud), haw, (thud)." I turned back to the ragwort.

"Oi, come here kid," he yelled. I ignored him. "Come 'ere!" he said even louder. I turned around.

"What do you want Oil?"

"Just come 'ere. You're working here ya gotta do what I say."

"That's right," someone growled from the other side of the car. It wasn't right, I was working for their father, but I lowered the sprayer and walked over anyway.

Oil wasn't wearing a shirt and there were greasy

marks on his shoulders from his hair. I could see Scuz sneering at me in the background.

"Hot work isn't it Smiffy," leered Oil, a cigarette hanging out of his mouth.

"Yeah it is," I answered, feeling like I did a couple of years ago when a bully used to steal my lunch at school.

Oil looked over at Scuz. "Hey poor Smiffy's hot Scuz, better give 'im a drink, aye."

"Yeah, it's firsty work," sneered Scuz. He reached among the cigarette packets on the floor and pulled out a half empty bottle of Coke.

"Here ya go mate," he said to me and passed the bottle over. "'Ave a drink."

The bottle was cold in my hands. I didn't want to annoy these two so I uncapped it and took a swig. As soon as it touched my lips I knew it wasn't Coke. I spat it onto the drive but it left a foul taste in my mouth.

"Haw, haw, haw," laughed Oil.

"Aw, Smiffy doesn't like rum," taunted Scuz.

"He's only a boy, it's a man's drink really," laughed Oil.

I threw the bottle back in the car and walked back

to the fence. It must have spilt because there was an "Oi!" from Scuz. "You . . . little . . . bastard," yelled Oil.

Suddenly the car roared to life, wheels spinning on the gravel road. It tore up the drive, gravel spraying the ground behind it. A stone slapped me in the back of the calf and a shower of little ones sprayed my back.

"Bloody mongrels," I swore and gave them a finger. I could hear Oil hooting and laughing out his window.

My calf was bruised but I limped back to the sprayer and carried on, trying to ignore it. Before long my shoulders hurt too so I didn't take quite as much notice of my leg. I tried to think of the money I was earning. By twelve o'clock I reckoned I had nearly twenty-three dollars. I'd brought my lunch with me so I went down to the creek to eat it. I could hear a stereo at the house and once Oil laughed, it was an ugly sound.

It was a long hot afternoon spraying ragwort, but at least Oil and Scuz didn't bother me any more. At about two o'clock I heard doors slamming and the black car tore out of the driveway, leaving a cloud of dust. I was glad they were gone, it made me uncomfortable when I could hear them at the house.

At five o'clock I finished the last tank of spray for the day. I was absolutely stuffed so I sat down in the sun for a minute before I took the sprayer back to the house. It felt great not to be using my aching muscles for a while.

The Buzzard was sitting on an old car seat at the front of the house. I walked over to him. He was sitting very still but he seemed to be watching me. I found out it was his blind eye when I dropped the sprayer on the ground. "Hah," he squawked, legs and arms flying in all directions. He grabbed a stick that was lying next to him and started waving it around. It took a moment before he saw me. "By the powers," he scowled, "don't go sneaking up on an old man like that, you're worse than those boys of mine, scaring me all the time."

"Sorry Mr Harnett," I said, trying to hold down a laugh.

"Right, ummm . . . ahhh, you've finished then, for the day?"

"Yeah I have. I worked seven-and-a-half hours, do you want me to write that down somewhere?"

“No, that’s alright. I’ll remember what days you were here.”

“You won’t forget?” I asked. “That’s a bit over fifty-five dollars today.”

“What! What are ya talking about?” cried The Buzzard waving his stick around. “You thieving young bugger, I said I was paying seven-fifty a day, there’s no way you’re getting fifty-five dollars.”

“But,” I stammered. “But I said seven-fifty.”

“Right,” he jabbed the stick towards me. “Seven-fifty, that’s the rate, we said nothing about paying you by the hour.”

Seven-fifty for the day, for all those hours. I couldn’t believe it, but here he was, jumping up and down in front of me. “You young blokes, trying to rip me off, an old man like me, it’s disgusting.”

“But Mr Harnett . . .”

“Don’t you ‘but’ me.” The Buzzard reached into his pocket, pulled out a crumpled five dollar note and a few coins and waved his hand towards me. “There, there’s your money, take it and get out, get off my land.”

I reached out for the money, but something stopped me – if I took it I was saying that was all I was worth, a few dollars for a whole day slaving out in the sun.

I shoved my hand back in my overalls and walked away.

"Here, take your money." He threw it down behind me. I heard the coins scatter on the path but I kept going.

After the Harnetts I enjoyed feeding Mr Hunterville's dogs. They were the nicest animals I had to deal with all day.

9
Payback Time

"That thieving old crook," growled Mum when I told her about what happened with The Buzzard. "I've got a good mind to go round there and break his other leg."

Vinny had come around to visit too. He looked at Mum in awe. "Remind me never to get on the wrong side of your Mum," he whispered.

"You're telling me," I answered, picking the fur off a tennis ball.

Meanwhile Mum had picked up the phone and dialled the Harnett's number.

She held the phone for a moment, tapping the floor with her foot, then smiled grimly when someone answered.

"What kind of a name's 'Oil'?"

Pause.

"I don't care what anyone calls you, Oil's a ridiculous name, put your father on." I shuddered. If Oil knew that was my mother I'd be in for it next time he saw me.

"Mr Harnett, I believe you only offered to pay my son seven-dollars-fifty for seven-and-a-half hours work today."

Pause.

"Yes it is Mrs Smith and I think that's ridiculous. If you can't get those pillocks of yours to work you can't expect my son to do it for the pittance that you offered him. What kind of a name is 'Oil' anyway?"

Pause.

"I am a woman Mr Harnett and I'll speak to you any way I like. If I was a man I'd probably go round there right now and sort you out."

Pause.

"Well you're an ignorant tight-fisted old git. Don't you think this thing is going to end here."

Mum slammed the phone down, she was red in the face and a little vein on her temple was throbbing. I put the kettle on and made her an extra strong cup of coffee while she marched around the kitchen muttering under her breath.

"I'm sorry Davin," she said when she'd calmed down a little. "I can't do anything right now, we're shearing for the next couple of days. I'll have a think about what we can do about that old git." Mum finished her coffee and went through to her office.

"Saw Dessy today," said Vinny as soon as Mum walked out the door. He had a new haircut and it was all slicked back with gel. It looked pretty cool.

"Yeah," I said, trying not sound too interested.

"Yeah," he sat back and put his feet on the table. "She's going to the movies with me tomorrow."

"Is she?" I asked, disappointed.

"Yeah, well Tu and Tammy are coming too, but I asked Dessy specially and she said she'd come. I'm sure something's going to happen, my stars said, 'Look forward to a change in fortunes.'"

"Man I wish I could have a change in fortunes."

"You're not wrong," said Vinny, "I'd seriously think about that wrecking business if I were you."

"Get out of here," I said, throwing the tennis ball at him.

"Or you could start horse breaking but you'd have to be careful about who gets broken first, you or the horse."

"Right!" I got up, but Vinny was too quick and ducked out the door. I didn't chase him, I just locked the door.

The next day was a scorcher. It was warm when Matt, Mr Tawhiti and the gang turned up, but by ten o'clock in the morning it was stinking hot. Mum and I were bringing the sheep up and dagging the few dirty ones when Vinny turned up. He was frantically motioning for me to come over so I walked across the yard.

"What's up?"

"I just saw the perfect way to get the Harnetts back," said Vinny excitedly.

"How?"

"Well, you know how they've got all those watermelons out in front of their place?"

"Yeah," I answered.

"And you know how it's stinking hot and there's three shearing gangs in the district?"

"Yeah."

"And the Harnetts are away today?"

I talked to Matt at smoko time and he agreed to help out. I told him I'd write off the money he owed me if he did. Vinny helped out in the yards for the morning. He didn't really know what he was doing, and I don't think it sped the job up much, but at least it gave Mum and me something to laugh at. Matt asked Mr Tawhiti if he could borrow the van over lunch, he agreed and Mum said it was okay if we went with him. We didn't say where we were going.

As soon as the shearers knocked off for lunch Matt got the van and we raced up to the Harnetts. Vinny was right, nobody was home. Matt drove along the road fence and Vinny and I picked watermelons and pushed them in the door. I kept looking at the road, expecting to see a black Holden come roaring up. I felt a lot better with Matt there cos I wouldn't have dared to do it if it was just Vinny and me. In no time we had twenty big juicy melons.

Then we went around the woolsheds. It was so hot that everyone was sitting quietly in the shade. They were all surprised to see us and when we showed them fresh watermelons they thought it was great. The cooks usually got a few for smoko and some of the shearers bought some for their families.

We took the melons to our own shearing gang last. Mrs Tawhiti was cooking for them and she was rapt when she saw the melons. "I'll have six of those," she said. "We can have watermelon for smoko." She pointed to Mr Tawhiti. "He's the contractor, he'll fix you up."

"Ohhh," grumbled Mr Tawhiti as he fished around in his pockets for some money. He cheered up though when he took a huge slice out of the melon and ate it. "Good kai," he said, juice dribbling down his chin.

We made sixty dollars out of the watermelons, and Matt and Vinny insisted that I keep it because I was the one who got ripped off. "But I only lost fifty-two dollars," I argued.

"Come to the movies with us, that'll take care of the rest of the money," said Vinny.

"Great idea," agreed Matt.

Mum wasn't quite so impressed. When she saw

what we'd done, she guessed straight away where we'd got the melons from. "You should know better," she growled, staring at us. "What if they'd come back and caught you nicking their melons? Reckless goats, would have served the lot of you right."

"Wow," said Matt when she walked away. "The Swampwitch must be getting soft, a few years ago she would have given us a real rev."

"Aye?" asked Vinny. He wasn't used to Mum's outbursts.

"That was nothing, should see her when she's really wild," I said.

"Too right," said Matt, walking back over to the woolshed to start shearing again.

I fed the Hunterville dogs again that night. I couldn't believe I'd been so scared of them when I first went around there. I think that's why they were so vicious, because they sensed that I was afraid. Now if any of them got too close or started snarling I'd growl and raise my hand and they'd cower away into the kennels. I was the one in control.

Vinny came up to my place and we both went to the movies from there. Mrs Tawhiti picked us up in their van.

"I thought you asked Dessy to go to the movies?" I said when Vinny told me who was picking us up.

"No," he said, looking guilty. "Tu and Tammy asked me to go along and I asked Dessy if she was coming too."

We piled into the back of the van and Vinny told everyone about what had happened with the Harnetts and the watermelons. "Faaaaa," said Tu, Tammy and Dessy together.

"You guys have all the fun, we've just been mucking around at home," said Tu.

"And riding the horses," I said, looking at Dessy. She gave me a little smile and I grinned back.

"What's on at the movies?" asked Vinny.

"*Fire and Ice*," said Tammy. "It's about a guy trying to track down his wife and kids after a war."

"Boring," groaned Tu.

"No," said Vinny, "I think it sounds alright, if you're a romantic kind of guy." Tu and I cracked up laughing and Tammy put her fingers down her throat. Dessy looked embarrassed.

We got some ice creams and popcorn and went into the picture theatre. Vinny was first, he winked at me and sat where there were two empty seats. Tu was going to sit next to him but Vinny pushed him away, he was saving it for Dessy. I found four empty seats, but only sat on the third one in because I thought Dessy would sit next to Vinny. Tu and Tammy sat next to me. Dessy glanced at the seat that Vinny had saved but kept walking and sat in the end seat. I couldn't believe it. Desiree Supermodel Davidson was sitting next to me.

I looked behind us. I'd thought Mrs Tawhiti was going to visit her sister but she walked down the aisle and took the spare seat next to Vinny. I couldn't help smiling when I turned around.

The movie started slowly and I only had half my mind on it and half my mind on Desiree. I had a big container of popcorn and put it between us so that we could share some.

The movie started to get really tense, the wife and kid were being stalked by a vicious killer who was only just behind them. He was getting closer and closer, meanwhile Desiree was leaning in closer and closer to me. I couldn't tell whether my heart was beating faster because of Dessy or the movie.

Eventually the husband caught up with the family, but not before the vicious killer had them cornered in an explosives storeroom and was about to light a match and send them all into oblivion. My arm was holding the popcorn, then suddenly Desiree latched onto it with both hands. It was great, except that her fingernails were digging in quite hard. There was a huge fight at the end and every time the hero got hit Desiree dug her fingers in some more. It was a relief when the bad guy finally got pummelled.

Desiree must have suddenly realised what she was doing because she let go my arm and leant over, "I'm sorry, I didn't realise. Is your arm okay?" she rubbed it.

"Never felt better," I said, meaning every word, and she giggled.

After the movies we went to the takeaway bar and got a feed. Dessy sat next to me and we started talking about her, where she was from, what she did. She had lots of relatives with farms and went to one every holidays. That was why she could ride so well.

"Say that again," said Tammy. I'd nearly forgotten she was there, I was so wrapped up in what Desiree was saying. We got to my place first and I said "see ya" to everyone. Vinny gave me an evil look but Dessy flashed a smile and I forgot all about Vinny. I couldn't believe that someone like Dessy actually liked me.

10
A Dirty Sheep Plucker

"How's business?" asked Matt when he came around for dinner the next week. We were sitting outside while Mum was cooking.

"Not good," I grumbled. "No one's rung up all week. The only good thing is that Mr Hunterville got back and paid me. No-one else seems to want a hand."

Matt laughed. "They've probably heard your reputation, Davin the Destroyer, Carterton's answer to a tropical cyclone."

"Not funny," I glared at him.

"You'll have to find something else," said Matt.

"Like what? There's nothing around here and even if there was something in town Mum couldn't take me in there every day." I'd been grumpy all week. I just couldn't think of any way to make money.

"I dunno," said Matt, thinking.

I picked at a chip of wood on the end of the table.

"Know what you could do?" asked Matt.

"What?'

"You could pluck dead sheep."

"Urrrrr." I screwed up my face.

"The wool price is up," he said.

"Get it while it's hot," yelled Mum from the kitchen.

"Get 'em when they're green," grinned Matt.

I didn't get any calls the next morning, Mum reckoned it was great. "You can give us a hand cleaning out the dip and killing a couple of sheep for the house."

Those jobs were just about as gross as plucking sheep, and I wouldn't get paid. "I'm already doing something." I said, miserably.

"What?"

"I'm going to pluck some sheep, Matt reckons there's some money in it."

Mum raised her eyebrows then smiled cruelly. "I'm sure that'll be a lot more fun."

I got my overalls and a big black rubbish bag. I was just about out the door when I remembered something else, there were some rubber gloves under the kitchen sink. Matt showed me once how he could blow them up to look like a cow's udder. I grabbed the gloves and started walking out the back of the farm. It was hot and I soon had a sweat up.

The first dead sheep I saw looked quite fresh. Its guts were blown up but it hadn't gone green yet. It was lying on a hillside. I walked up to it and pushed it with the toe of my gumboot but it was stiff and hardly gave at all.

I took a deep breath. "Righto sheep, better make this easy." I stretched both the gloves over my hands then reached down and grabbed a piece of wool. I pulled it. It didn't come out. I pulled again, harder this time. Still nothing happened. I gripped the wool with both hands and tugged it really hard, I felt something giving. The next moment the whole sheep came unstuck and came towards me with a jerk.

"Arrrgh!" I yelled, letting go. The sheep skidded down onto my feet and I lost my balance. I tripped over backwards, with the dead sheep on top of my legs.

I scrambled out of there at the speed of light. There was dead sheep slime all over the legs of my overalls. "Yuck!" I spat onto the grass, then grabbed a handful of long grass and wiped most of the slime off my overalls, they were still disgusting but there wasn't anything I could do. The dead sheep just lay there, I couldn't bring myself to touch it again.

I walked for half an hour without seeing any sheep. I sat down and wiped my face with my overall sleeve. It was overcast and muggy and I was dying to get home or at least find a trough to duck my head into. I spotted a sheep carcass in a gully and tramped over, it was really ripe. The patches of skin you could see were green and it stank. I had to hold my breath to get anywhere near it.

This time I stood back as far as I could and grasped some wool. It just came out in my gloves, I hardly even had to pull. Then I remembered Matt's words, 'Get 'em while they're green'. He wasn't joking, that was the best way to pluck sheep.

I stuffed the handful into the rubbish bag and started pulling out fistfuls of wool which came out at the skin, leaving green hide underneath. The stink was terrible and I ended up breathing out of my mouth instead of my nose so it didn't smell so much.

The sheep looked really stupid when I'd done the top. It was green and completely naked, even more naked than they were just after shearing. I saw a bit of wool poking out from underneath. "Of course," I muttered, there was still as much wool on the other side. I grabbed a leg and started to turn it over. I had it halfway over when the stench hit me – it smelled like dog shit, vomit and rotten eggs all mixed together. I looked down, the sheep and the ground were crawling, the whole lot was covered in a moving blanket of shiny white maggots.

I dropped the leg, I could feel something wriggling on my hand. "Yaaaahhhh," I leapt back and ground my hand into the dirt then rubbed it back and forwards in the grass until it was a dirty green colour. I felt sick in my stomach and kind of shaky. I vowed not to turn over any more dead sheep.

I found another four sheep before I went home.

One was too fresh to pluck, there were two good ones and one that was so rotten that if you pulled the wool on its leg the whole leg was likely to come off. So I left that one as it was. I made sure I knew where the fresh sheep were and walked home with a bag of wool over my shoulder.

"Whewwww," said Mum when I walked in the door, "you smell like a morgue, leave those overalls outside and get in the shower, use plenty of soap too."

"Yeah righto." I usually hated having a shower but today was a bit different.

We had cold roast mutton with rice salad for tea. There was fresh mint sauce to go with it. The sauce was like green jelly with lumps in it. It looked like parts of the rotten sheep that I'd seen.

"You're looking pale tonight," said Mum.

"Mmmm," I said, thinking if I opened my mouth too wide I'd throw up.

"Not feeling well?" she asked.

I shook my head.

"Have some meat, it'll make you feel better," said Mum.

I bolted to the toilet, my stomach felt like it was going to leap out of my throat. I didn't throw up but

I got really close. When I got back to the kitchen Mum had put some glad wrap over tea.

"It's okay if you don't feel well, you can have that for tea tomorrow," she said.

I couldn't tell her that her tea looked like rotten sheep, Mum's sensitive about her cooking. I decided that I'd have to get up later and have a midnight snack of peanut butter sandwiches. I could feed tea to the dogs so that I wouldn't get it tomorrow night.

The next day I plucked the rest of the dead sheep on our place. I rang up Mr Hunterville and Mr Todd and they both said that I could pluck any dead sheep thcy had as long as I buried the carcasses while I was there. It looked like my sheep-plucking business could be a success.

I spent the rest of the day working my way towards Mr Todd's. He had plenty of sheep and Mum always says, "Where there's live ones there's gotta be dead ones." It was true too, except that you had to walk a long way to get to them.

Finally, I had a full bag of wool so I headed off home. That was okay, except that it stank and flies kept buzzing around my head. I was hoping that I wouldn't meet anyone when Tammy and Desiree trotted around the track on the horses. I'd forgotten that Dessy was riding Firebrand. It was too late to hide, I knew I'd have to talk to them even if I did smell like a grave robber.

"G'day," I said, standing well off the track so they couldn't smell me.

"Phewwww," said Tammy, "something stinks around here. Did you drop your guts Davin Smith?"

I felt my face going red straight away. "I . . . I've been plucking dead sheep."

Desiree looked surprised, "Why do you wanna do that?"

"For fun," laughed Tammy.

I gave Tammy a dirty look. "The wool's worth money, I'm going to sell it."

"Oh," said Desiree, screwing up her nose.

"That's what you've been doing. Are you going to come up to the waterhole tomorrow? Vinny and Connor and everyone's coming, should be good fun," said Tammy.

"Yep," I said.

"Make sure you have a wash first though, don't want to pollute the river," Tammy laughed. "C'mon Dessy, it stinks around here," she kicked her horse and cantered away. Desiree looked like she was going to say something but Firebrand was pulling at the bit so she gave him his head and cantered after Tammy.

"Damn," I muttered, it was impossible to be cool and suave when you're dressed in overalls and gum-boots and smelled like a rubbish dump. Oh well, I thought, I'll be cleaner tomorrow.

11
A Bright Idea

I was happy to give myself the next day off. There were a few carcasses on Mr Todd's place that needed another day out in the sun so they'd be just ripe for the plucking.

I saw Vinny ahead of me as I biked down the road on my way to the waterhole. I hadn't seen him since we went to the movies. "Hey Vinny!" I yelled.

He looked around, he must have seen me, but he sped up.

"Vinny!" I yelled, and he went even faster. Vinny may have had a flash mountain bike and all the riding gear but I had Matt's old bike, a road-racing fourteen speed. I knew I could catch him so I stood up on my pedals and started chasing.

Vinny crouched down over his seat and wound his pedals around like crazy but he wasn't getting away. Gradually I closed down the gap until I was by his back wheel. Vinny didn't even look at me.

"Oi!" I yelled. "Slow down."

"Bugger off!" he growled.

"What's your problem?"

Vinny grabbed his brakes, and skidded to a halt, luckily I was to the side of him otherwise I would have crashed into his rear wheel. As it was I sailed five metres past him before I managed to stop.

I turned and glared back at him. "Mate, you could have killed me."

"Serve you right," he barked.

I was amazed, "What have I done to you?"

"You're a back stabber, running around with Desiree when you knew I liked her."

That really hacked me off. "And when did you ask me if I liked her, aye? Did you ever think that Dipstick

Davin might stand a chance? You're not the only one in the world, Vinny Mattiasovich." Vinny's jaw must have dropped a foot. I'd never seen him lost for words before.

"I've got a life too!" I pushed off with one foot and rode on ahead. I didn't look back at him.

Vinny caught up again a kilometre up the road. He biked next to me and didn't say anything for quite a while. That's really unusual for Vinny. "So you like Dessy too?" he asked quietly (also unusual for Vinny).

I nodded.

"Why didn't you say so?"

"Because you were too busy raving on about how much you liked her," I said. It was quiet again except for the whirring of our wheels.

"I suppose I was being a bit of an idiot," he said eventually.

"Yup."

We biked for a few minutes in silence. Finally I couldn't help laughing.

"What's so funny?" asked Vinny.

"Your chat-up line at the movie." I tried to imitate him. "I think it sounds alright, if you're a romantic kind of guy."

Vinny gave an embarrassed grin. "It does sound a bit corny doesn't it?"

"Didn't do you much good either," I chuckled.

"What do you use then?" asked Vinny. "It seems to work pretty well."

I shrugged my shoulders. "I don't have any lines, I just talk like I always do."

Vinny thought about that for a while.

I laughed and imitated him again. "You play a really good game of touch, are you a Libra?"

"Piss off!" he tried to squirt me with his water bottle but I laughed and biked away from him, keeping just out of squirting range. Vinny was laughing too, it felt good.

Everyone else was at the waterhole when we got there. It was a deep, sandy pool in the river with a sheer bank on one side and a sandy beach on the other. The bank was nearly vertical but the summer before we'd all come down for a week and made steps up to a really awesome diving platform. We'd also put a rope swing off an overhanging tree so that we could swing out over the river and drop into the water. We'd muck around diving and swinging for ages then lie on the beach and bake in the sun. It was the best spot on the river.

Everyone saw us as we walked up. "Keep outta here!" called Tammy. "You'll stink the place out."

"Yeah, there's no dead sheep down here," yelled Tu.

"Yeeeeeha!" called Connor as he let go of the swing and splashed into the hole. It was funny how he lost his stutter when he was doing something like that. I couldn't see Desiree but suddenly Tammy screamed and splashed. "There's an eel, there's an eel!"

Desiree bobbed up next to her, giggling. She saw Vinny and me, but disappeared again as Tammy ducked her. Vinny and I dived into the water in our shorts.

"Bet I can get higher on the swing!" called Tu.

"Like hell," said Vinny.

"Come on then." Tu swam over to the swing and we all followed. We stayed on the swings and diving platform for ages. Tu could get the most air as he came off the swing but Tammy always did the biggest bombs.

Connor was the king of the diving platform, he could do forward and backward flips.

"I reckon I could do a forward flip," said Tu.

"G . . . go on," stammered Connor.

"Alright then, I will."

Tu was trying to clown around when he stood on the platform but we could all tell that he was nervous. He dived off and did a weird sideways twist. He hit the water with his back down and his face screwed up. It made a wicked slapping sound and his whole back was one big red mark when he came out of the water.

"D . . . d . . . didn't quite nail it T . . . T . . . Tu. Have another g . . . go," called Connor, grinning.

"Grrrrrrr," growled Tu.

"It's alright bro," said Tammy, slapping him on the back. He yelped and pushed her in but she grabbed his shorts and took him with her. We all went over to the sandy beach and relaxed out in the sun, but not before Tammy had made us put some sunblock on.

"I don't need this," said Tu. "Give it to those two pale fellas over there."

"Wanna fight about it," growled Tammy. Tu groaned and let her rub some sunblock on. She made the rest of us put it on too.

We heard a tractor drive past on the road.

"I . . . I . . . is your Mum getting another c . . . c . . . car?" asked Connor.

"Yeah, it must be a bummer going everywhere on your tractor," added Tammy.

"She should enter that competition in town," said Tu.

"What competition?" I asked, sitting up.

"Y . . . you know, you've g . . . gotta hold your hand on the c . . . car."

"Yeah, the last one with their hand left on wins the car," finished Tu.

I was getting excited. Vinny and I exchanged a glance. "Can anyone enter?" I asked.

"Yeah, but you've gotta pay $150.00. That's how they raise the money to do it."

I did some mental maths. With the $70.00 from feeding the dogs and $52.00 from watermelons I had $122.00. The wool I'd plucked would take that up to $150.00.

"I'm going to enter," I said.

"Yeah right." Tammy laughed.

Vinny raised his eyebrows at me.

"For real?" asked Tu.

"Yeah, I'm going to win that car for Mum," I said.

Everyone sat up.

"They had one of those up near home," said Dessy. "It lasted for days."

"Come on you guys, you're dreaming." Tammy looked me in the eyes. "Davin, I'm not running you down mate, but you know what you're like. I've never met anyone as clumsy. You've got more chance of accidentally setting off a nuclear bomb than you have of winning a car."

Connor nodded sadly and Tu murmured in agreement. Vinny gazed at me for a moment. "I reckon you can do it."

I knew that I could, I had to.

12
Fighting Fit

"When's it on?" asked Vinny.

"Saturday, it's at McGreedy's Car Yard," said Tu.

"Not much time," commented Tammy.

Vinny grinned. "It's not like he has to train or anything."

We talked about it for ages, everyone had ideas except for Tu. He was lying back on the grass and falling asleep.

Desiree saw him, put a finger to her lips then

reached over to where Tu had left his sandshoes. She pulled one of his socks out of it. The sock must have been white once but now it was a dirty grey colour. It looked damp and sweaty. Dessy rolled it into a ball and held it beside Tu's nose. He groaned in his sleep, screwed up his face and opened his mouth.

"Gross," said Vinny. Desiree shoved the sock into Tu's mouth then sat straight down and tried to look innocent.

"Uhhhhh," groaned Tu, and his eyes flew open. "Uhhhhh, uhhhhh." He ripped the sock out of his mouth and started spitting on the ground, holding his throat. "Urrrgh," he cried, racing down to the river to take great gulps of water and then spitting them out.

We were laughing so hard we were all rolling around in the sand. Tu had a wild look in his eyes. "Which one of you mongrels poisoned me!" He stomped up, staring first at Vinny, then at Tammy. "I could of died, these things are lethal," he said. He must have got another whiff of socks because he started coughing and his eyes were watering.

"Call the ambulance," said Tammy, "I think he's going into shock."

"Nah, that's a waste of time, let's cut out the middle man and take him straight to the morgue," Vinny chuckled.

Tu threw the sock at Vinny, Tammy biffed Tu's other sock at him, then it broke into a full scale riot with everyone throwing sand and scragging each other into the water. I tried to duck Dessy but she started scratching and pinching, then Tammy helped her out and I was the one that got ducked. It was awesome fun.

Finally we collapsed on the sand. "Hey, we could be your support crew for the Car Challenge," said Tu.

"Yeah, we could get your food and keep you awake and cheer for you," said Dessy.

"That'd be great," I grinned.

We made plans for the Great Car Challenge, in between fooling around in the waterhole.

"Too much," said Tammy as we were all about to leave. "You'll have the best crew in the whole competition, you still gotta hang onto that car though."

"No worries," I said, trying to sound more confident than I felt.

Vinny and I were biking home again when we heard a car rumbling along the road, the sound was familiar. "Aw no," I moaned as the black Holden careered around the corner in front of us while Vinny and I pulled over to the extreme left of the road. The car came closer and closer but I couldn't see the driver through the dark tinted windscreen. I turned my head away, hoping they wouldn't recognise me.

The cars tyres screeched, there was a puff of smoke and the vehicle skidded sideways, blocking the whole road. Vinny braked hard to avoid it, but I was that close to him that I rammed into his bike. We toppled sideways as I heard the car doors bursting open.

My shoulder and hip struck the road together. I gasped, then a hand gripped the back of my t-shirt and yanked me to my feet. I opened my eyes and looked straight into a greasy black moustache.

"Gotcha," growled Oil. I was gasping for air and got a face full of his hot, stinking breath. It smelt like our pig scraps when I hadn't put them out for a week.

I could hear Vinny in the background. "Get off me you ignorant sod. You try anything and I'll sue you!"

“Let ’im go,” barked Oil, “we’ve got the one we want.” He lifted me completely off the ground and shook me. “Been complaining to Mum have we Smiffy? Making you work too hard. Mum gave me a hard time about my name, I think we better give you a hard time.”

“You leave him alone,” called Vinny in the background. I knew I was in for it now. I closed my eyes and hoped that it wouldn’t be too painful.

“Give him ‘ere,” said Scuz. I could hear his steel capped boots thudding across the concrete. “I’ll sort him out.”

“Let Davin go or you’ll lose your keys,” shouted Vinny.

I opened my eyes and twisted my head. Vinny was standing by the car, jiggling the keys in his hand. “If you don’t let him go I’m biffing your keys in there.” He pointed towards a hay paddock off to the side of the road.

“You drop those now, dickhead,” cried Scuz.

Vinny pulled his arm back as if he was going to throw the keys. Scuz moved towards him.

“Stay there,” growled Oil, letting me go.

“Dav,” called Vinny. “Pick up the bikes and bring

them over here. Oil, if either of you move, your keys are history."

I did what Vinny asked, bringing the bikes over. "Right," he said, staring at Oil and Scuz as if they were something that he'd picked up from the bottom of his sneakers. "Stay right there." He took his bike off me and wheeled it up the road, keeping an eye on Scuz and Oil while I followed him.

"What are you going to do?" I whispered. "If they get the keys back they'll run us down."

"I know," hissed Vinny, "just do what I tell you." We'd wheeled our bikes to the top of a rise, about thirty metres away from Oil and Scuz.

"Give us the keys," growled Oil, starting to move towards us.

"Go!" yelled Vinny as he threw the keys as far into the hay paddock as he could. I got on my bike and pedalled furiously, Vinny right beside me. We could hear Oil and Scuz cursing and pounding down the road behind us, but it was downhill and we were far too fast for them.

"Yeeha!" called Vinny, letting go of his handlebars and waving his arms.

"You're a legend!" I yelled.

There was a chance that they'd find the keys while we were still on the road so we rode home as fast as we could. We took turns going first while the other one slip-streamed behind. "Good luck," called Vinny as he turned off.

"See you at McGreedy's on Saturday," I yelled.

My legs felt like they were burning, I heard a noise on the road behind me. I didn't even turn around, I ignored the pain and pumped my legs as fast as I could. I could feel the sweat forming on the back of my t-shirt. A motorbike roared past me, banking over as it took the turn.

Matt was taking his leathers off when I pulled in a few minutes later. "Mate," he said, "looked like you were in a hurry."

"Got that right."

"Did it have anything to do with a couple of hoods I saw rooting around in a hay paddock?"

"Were they still at it?" I grinned.

"Like pigs in a wallow," said Matt. "If you had anything to do with it you better keep your head down for a while, they'll have it in for you."

13
Competition

I hadn't told Mum about the Car Challenge, I wanted to surprise her and get Matt to drive us home in a new car. I'd arranged for Vinny and me to be staying at Matt's place for the weekend. That way she wouldn't know what was going on.

McGreedy's Car Yard was a hive of activity. There were flags and banners everywhere, even a live band on a stage. All the cars had 'Bargain' and 'Sale' and 'Reduced' signs on them, although Vinny reckoned that they were all more expensive than they had been the week before. There were hundreds of people milling around and Vinny and I had to push our way through the crowds to get to where the Great Car Challenge was happening.

"That's the car," said Vinny, pointing to where a shiny red Commodore was roped off from the crowd. It was a big sleek car with a wing on the back and paintwork so shiny that you could see the reflections of the crowd in it. I could just picture Mum's face if we turned up at home with her new car. She'd be stunned. I thought that would be the ideal time to tell her about leaving a certain handbrake off.

Vinny saw Dessy and the Tawhitis in the crowd and pushed and bumped his way towards them. He made sure I was behind him and that I didn't get knocked around. "Can't let our man get hurt," he said.

"Thanks for coming guys," I said when we got there.

"What excuse did you use so you could stay in town?"

Tu looked at Tammy and she raised her eyebrows. "You tell him," she said.

Tu looked glum. "Didn't need an excuse. Aunty Hepi's entered in the competition and Mum made us come in and support her. We're staying at her place."

"Oh," I said.

"Doesn't mean we can't support you too," said Dessy.

"Yeah," mumbled Tu, "it's just that she really needs the car. Uncle Sonny's in hospital and she hasn't got a car to go and visit him. It means a lot to her."

"Man, you don't have to tell him that," said Vinny angrily.

"Doesn't matter guys," I said. "There's heaps of people entered, it probably won't come down to me and your Aunty Hepi."

"That's true," said Tu. "When one of you drops out we can go on supporting the other one." Tammy nodded in agreement.

I went over to register and pay my money. I was at the desk when I heard a commotion in the crowd. I looked over and saw Oil's greasy head appear then disappear towards the car. He was followed by Scuz and a dog that was even more vicious than he was, a huge snarling rottweiler that strained at its leash. Great, I thought, they were all I needed. The butterflies were starting in my stomach and my hands were sweaty. I handed over the money and signed the entry form, I was too nervous to even read it.

Mr McGreedy was a huge man. Even in the heat he wore a sportscoat and a tiny, bright bow tie. Sweat ran down his face in trickles and gathered in the wrinkles on his chin. He hauled himself onto the stage, waddled to the microphone and cleared his throat with a great rumble. The crowd hushed.

"Welcome ladies and gentlemen to McGreedy's Car Yard for the start of McGreedy's Great Car Challenge. In five minutes exactly these brave competitors will place their hands on this beautiful pre-loved Commodore. The last one remaining with a hand on the vehicle will drive away with this gem of a car, only a genuine thirty thousand kilometres on the clock and one elderly female owner. Great to see all the supporters here at McGreedy's. While the competition's under way please feel free to have a look at some of the fantastic deals we've got going for the duration of the Great Car Challenge. Take this lovely . . . "

I pushed my way back through the crowd to where the gang was. Connor slapped me on the shoulder. "G . . . good luck."

Tu shoved a banana towards me and Tammy gave me a small bag of oranges. "Gotta keep your energy up," she said.

Vinny frowned. "How's he supposed to peel these with one hand on the car?"

"I'll peel them," Dessy said. "He can have them during his breaks."

"B . . . breaks?" asked Connor.

"Yeah, I read Aunty Hepi's entry form, they get five minutes off every hour for refreshments and to use those port-a-loos and stuff."

Tu laughed. "Lucky it's not Tammy, she'd never be out of the toilet in five minutes."

The speakers crackled in the background. "Could all competitors for McGreedy's Great Car Challenge please take their places in the Challenge Ring please."

"Good luck."

"Do it man."

"G . . . Go hard."

Everyone slapped me on the back and I headed over to the ring. It was filling up quickly with all sorts of people, all wanting to win the car. I caught a glimpse of Cowboy Todd in the ring and the Tawhiti's Aunty Hepi, a big smiling woman. There was an uproar in the crowd as Oil shoved his way into the ring, Scuz and the rottweiler behind him.

Mr McGreedy pushed through, put a chair by the front of the car, stood on it and lifted a megaphone. The police chief stood next to him. "Congratulations to all fifty of our brave competitors. The competition will start in one minute. I hope you've all read the rules, Inspector Dawson will be in charge of disqualifications. Anyone removing their hands will be immediately disqualified. Please find a place on the car."

There was a surge of people towards the car. I was at the back of the ring, trying to avoid Scuz. When I got to the car both sides of it were packed solidly with competitors.

"Get in there Dav," I heard Tammy yelling from the crowd. I spotted the nearest gap and plunged into it.

I bumped into someone, knocking their arm, and something fell to the ground. I ignored it until I could feel the slick metal of the car under my fingers then looked down. It was a tube of super glue, lying on the ground. I couldn't work out why it was there until I saw large, greasy fingers clamp around it. Oil stared up at me. "Why you . . . " he growled, but I spun around and got out of there before he could say any more.

"Twenty seconds," called Mr McGreedy.

I desperately looked around the ring but there was no space to squeeze into. I tried a half gap and got pushed back again by a tough-looking blonde woman wearing leather pants.

"Ten seconds, nine, eight," called Mr McGreedy. My heart was racing, I had to find a gap.

". . . seven, six, five . . ." There was just a solid wall of people in front of me. I was going to lose before I'd even started.

"Go Dav, underneath the car," yelled Vinny.

". . . four, three . . ." I dived amongst the legs and squeezed through till I was completely under the car.

". . . two, one . . ." I hooked my arm over the driveshaft.

"Go." I sighed. I'd made it.

14
The Trial

It was hard to tell what was going on from under the car. All I could see were a hundred shoes and an occasional glimpse of the crowd behind them. One pair of men's shoes was getting closer and closer to a woman's boots, the boots shuffled away until they were trapped against a pair of gumboots. The boots tapped up and down, more and more quickly until one of them jumped up and stomped the shoes on the toe. From then on the woman's boots had plenty of room.

The first hour passed quickly. Twice I saw pairs of shoes trip, then trudge off back into the crowd. Some shoes tapped and shuffled, others were still. Several stripped off to leave just bare feet standing around the car.

Eventually a car horn sounded and all the shoes shifted away for a break. All except for one pair of dirty black combat boots.

"There he is," called Vinny. I looked over and the gang were all on their knees, grinning over at me.

"Hi guys," I waved and slid out from under the car. I looked across it and wasn't surprised to see Oil still touching the bonnet, he couldn't move. I pulled a face and he raised his middle finger back at me.

"What's going on here?" bellowed Inspector Dawson, striding over to Oil.

"He's a bit stuck, Ossifer," I said.

The inspector glared at me for a moment before shifting his attention to Oil. "Stuck?" he asked.

"Super glue," I said.

Inspector Dawson glared at me again and I moved away a little. "Is that true Adrian?" he asked, staring at Oil. I couldn't believe his proper name was Adrian.

No wonder everyone called him Oil, it suited him much better.

Oil didn't seem worried. "Nothin' in the rules against it," he sneered.

The inspector frowned and marched back to talk to Mr McGreedy. I stepped outside the ropes and the gang got to work. Tu pulled out a deckchair and Connor pushed me into it, then started pounding my shoulders. Dessy gave me a drink before she went with Tu and Tammy to see how their Aunty Hepi was getting on.

Vinny shoved a small jar of smelling salts under my nose. It felt like the inside of my nostrils was being burnt out. I pulled back, but he followed my nose with the jar. "Owww." I choked, spitting my drink out and struggling to get away, but I couldn't because of Connor's punishing massage. Instead I grabbed Vinny's hand and shoved the salts under his nose. He got a good whiff and his eyes glazed over then came clear again. "Wow!" he said.

"No more," I told him.

He nodded vaguely and looked into the jar. "That's pretty wild stuff!" And he took another whiff.

It seemed like no time at all before Mr McGreedy

called everyone back to the car. This time I got in early and had a good spot by the boot, well away from Oil.

"Right," announced Inspector Dawson. "One of you has chosen to go against the spirit of fair play and glue themselves to this vehicle. The rules mention nothing about such behaviour and so I am unable to disqualify this unsavoury character. But be warned, if that person (he frowned in Oil's direction) or anyone else breaks any of the rules they'll be instantly disqualified." He glared at the competitors. "Carry on," he said, then turned and marched to the front of the car.

I was opposite Aunty Hepi, who saw me and gave me a nod and a smile. She didn't look tense at all, she was talking to the woman next to her as if she was an old friend she'd met on the street, not someone she was in competition against.

There were all types of people around the car, some were talking to each other, others were glancing around at the crowd. One older woman was standing really stiff and holding rosary beads. Her lips were moving but she wasn't making any sound and every now and then she'd move onto the next bead. A younger woman was reading a book but she had to put it on the boot to change the page, it looked really awkward.

I saw Vinny standing behind her in the crowd. I couldn't make it out but he seemed to have a spider or something crawling on the back of his right shoulder. One of the other competitors saw it too, an old Maori guy. He caught Vinny's eye and wriggled his shoulder. Vinny looked confused so the guy wriggled his shoulder again but Vinny still didn't seem to get it, he shrugged instead. Then the guy tapped the back of his shoulder with his right hand, the one that had been on the car.

Inspector Dawson walked over and gripped the man by the shoulder. "Sorry sir, you let go of the vehicle, you're disqualified." I looked over to where Vinny had been and he was sneaking away, taking a rubber spider off his shoulder as he went. The Maori guy scowled and looked into the crowd but he couldn't spot Vinny.

A few more people dropped off the car that hour, mainly for doing silly things like brushing their hair back or having a scratch. One guy just went to look at his watch and let go of the car.

I saw Oil quite often as I looked around. No-one would stand very close to him cos there was something about him that turned people away. He had a sly smile on his face. It made me feel sick, I knew he had more dirty tricks than just the super glue.

The second hour came up quickly, and when the horn sounded everyone spread out again. Tu, Tammy and Desiree had gone into town but Vinny and Connor were there. As soon as I was in the deckchair I grabbed Vinny by the arm. "Hang on a sec Vinny, what was that thing with the spider?"

He grinned. "Just helping out."

"Well don't," I said. "If they catch you I'll get disqualified, that's not going to help me out at all."

Vinny pulled his arm away and frowned. "Don't you want my help then?"

"Course I do, you're doing a great job with the support crew. I could even win this thing." Vinny was still looking down.

"Is that okay?" I asked.

"Yeah," he shrugged, "alright. It was a pretty good trick with the spider though."

I had to smile. "Yeah but I nearly patted my shoulder to show you where it was."

He grinned. "Serve you right for having dishonest mates."

We were into our third hour now and it was getting hard to keep my hand on the car. Once I nearly moved it to scratch my ear but caught myself just in time. Other people were having the same problem, ten had already dropped out.

The time passed slowly so I talked to some of the people near me. There was a farmer on one side who was really worried that the competition would take too long because he'd have to go and milk his cows. The woman on the other side had two kids that she wanted to tell me all about. When she started raving on about potty training I had to tell her that it wasn't something that I was into. She seemed quite put out.

There was always someone there during the breaks, giving me oranges, a massage or just talking to me. I had to go for a leak in one of the breaks and I suddenly realised something. I rushed over to Vinny.

"Mate, Oil's stuck to the car right?"

"Yeah." said Vinny.

"Well he can't go to the toilet."

"Right."

"He's gotta go sometime, he'll have to get cut off the car or something."

Vinny frowned. "I s'pose you're right."

"Course I am," I grinned. There was no way he could win. I smiled at him when I got back and kept an eye on his face. Somewhere near the fifth hour his face got really tense, the veins on his forehead stood out and he seemed to be biting his lip. This was it, I thought, he had to move.

I was wrong, near the end of the hour I looked at his face again and it was relaxed. I couldn't understand it until I looked under the car. There was a puddle running from his boots and draining away across the car yard. I screwed up my nose and looked at him in disgust but he sneered back. After that three people who had been standing next to him left. Oil's grin got bigger.

It steadily got later and the crowd thinned out. Matt and Vinny brought a pile of sleeping bags and a mattress over to sit on. The streetlights came on. Cowboy Todd started to grimace as he moved his weight from one leg to the other. It was obviously hurting and eventually he let go of the vehicle, shook his head and limped away.

Vinny and Matt brought me dinner at six o'clock. It was a sort of spaghetti bolognaise that Matt had made at his place.

"Good carbohydrate food," said Vinny.

"Yup," agreed Matt, "that'll keep your energy up."

Mum obviously hadn't taught Matt much about cooking. The spaghetti pieces were all stuck together and the mince had these big lumps all through it. I was pretty hungry though, and managed to eat nearly all of it in the five minute break.

We reached nine o'clock then ten, then eleven. Tu, Tammy, Desiree and Connor had to go and sleep at their Aunty's but Vinny and Matt stayed. Inspector Dawson was replaced by PC Pierce who hung around like a vulture. He had a torch that he used to spotlight people. He flashed the older woman with the rosary beads when she started praying under her breath, then she put her hand up to shield her eyes and he immediately disqualified her.

He was really suspicious of Oil, glancing at him constantly. I realised that he wasn't going to catch him out, it was physically impossible for Oil to take his hand off the car.

15
In the Dead of the Night

By midnight people at the car were starting to go to sleep. Their eyes would blink, then they'd rest against the car. They'd be struggling to keep upright. Finally they'd drop off for a few seconds while they were standing there. I saw several people do that. They'd be okay while they cat-napped, but when they woke up they'd rub their eyes or push themselves upright and lose contact with the car.

At two in the morning I was starting to feel sleepy

myself. I looked over at Matt and Vinny, but they were both asleep on the mattress. My eyelids were growing heavy and I knew I couldn't keep awake for much longer.

It was nearly time for a break. I looked blearily around and saw someone walking over, wrapped in a blanket and carrying a cup. It was Dessy. She grinned at me.

"Righto, time for a break," called PC Pierce. "Remember, only five minutes, any longer and you're out."

"G'day Dessy," I said. "I thought you'd gone back to Aunty Hepi's for a sleep."

"I did," she replied, handing me a hot cup of milky coffee. "I couldn't sleep and Mrs Tawhiti was coming down to see how it was going so I came along. I wanted to talk to you."

I slurped my coffee. "Mmmmm . . . "

"I'm going home tomorrow."

I nearly dropped the coffee, I didn't know what to say.

"I was only going to be staying for a few weeks. It's Mum's birthday and I've gotta go. I won't be coming back this summer."

"It . . . it seems like you've been around for ages,

I never even thought about you leaving," I said, looking at the ground.

"Me neither."

We stood there in silence for a moment. Dessy shifted awkwardly. "I . . . I really enjoyed getting to know you this summer. Even just a little bit."

I grinned. "I got a kick out of making a new friend too."

Dessy was playing with a thread on her blanket. "Just friends?"

"I . . . I don't know. If you'd been here longer would you have been my girlfriend?" I asked, my heart pounding.

Dessy showed her teeth in a smile. "I would have liked that."

She leant against one of the cars in the lot. "That's why I wanted to talk to you now, while no one's around, it's the only time we've been alone." She reached out and held my hand.

"Time's up, everyone back at the car," called PC Pierce. I was sure he hadn't given us five minutes. I gave Dessy's hand a squeeze. "Thanks."

"I better go, I'll see you tomorrow," said Dessy, holding my hand for a second longer.

“See you.” I walked back and held my hand on the car, watched suspiciously by PC Pierce. I was wide awake now, thinking about what Dessy had told me, thinking about her touch on my hand. There was no danger of falling asleep.

At about four o’clock in the morning I heard footsteps at the edge of the car yard, then a sharp whistle and a scrabbling of paws. A dark shape burst out of the shadows, white fangs bared.

“Look out!” I yelled as the rottweiler launched itself towards the back of the car, growling hoarsely. People screamed, pushing each other and tripping in their panic. I crouched at the front of the car and saw Aunty Hepi, frozen in horror, and Oil pulling frantically against the car. Everyone else was running.

The rottweiler was less than a metre away from a woman, saliva was dripping from its jaws and it was stretching for her. Suddenly it seemed to crash into an invisible wall. Its head was yanked back and it slammed back onto the yard, its breath escaping in one great whoosh. It lay on the ground, unconscious.

I recognised the dog instantly and looked over at Oil. He grinned at me with a fanatical gleam in his eye.

I saw PC Pierce crouched on the roof of a station wagon. "Shit!" he muttered, then seemed to remember that he was in charge. He got down and looked around uncertainly. "Um, right." He raised his voice. "No need to panic, everything's under control. Could everyone step back and place your hands on the vehicle. I'm sure we can sort this incident out."

"Hang on," scowled Oil, "it says in the rules that you can't take your hands off the car for any reason. They should be disqualified."

PC Pierce frowned. "Everyone stay right where you are." He stepped away and used his radio. Matt and Vinny had been woken by all the fuss and they joined the other spectators who had gathered around the ring. Within minutes Inspector Dawson and Mr McGreedy were at the yard. Someone checked the unconscious dog and found a rope attached to its collar. It was tied to the fence at the back of the yard. The dog started to come around, shaken and bewildered. PC Pierce was ordered to take it to the vet.

Inspector Dawson and Mr McGreedy were arguing over what to do. Finally Inspector Dawson stepped over to the crowd. "Ladies and gentlemen, I'm sorry but the rules were clear, anyone letting go of the vehicle is disqualified, no matter what the reason. All competitors are out, except for the three remaining at the car."

The rest of the competitors argued fiercely with him but he wouldn't change his mind. There were rules and he couldn't get around them. I glanced at Oil and Aunty Hepi, it was just the three of us.

At six o'clock that morning I was feeling really tired. Aunty Hepi was still smiling though and chatting away to Inspector Dawson, who had stayed on after he was called out. Aunty Hepi smiled over at me.

"You hanging in there boy?"

"Yeah," I said. "How come you're so wide awake?"

"Not the first time I've stayed up all night," she laughed and winked, then carried on chatting.

Oil, on the other hand, looked terrible. He was grimacing and I could see sweat on his forehead and dribbling down his face. He kept shifting from one foot to the other. Nobody came anywhere near him. A new puddle had formed by his boots and he stank.

As we approached the next break he got worse and worse, fidgeting and blinking, and he couldn't seem to stand still.

"Time for a break," called Inspector Dawson at seven

o'clock. This time Oil didn't just stand where he was. He leant away from the car and started to pull. The car rocked but he couldn't pull his hand off. Oil moaned, his eyes looked wild and he was shaky. He put both knees against the side of the car, leant his weight against it then pulled back as hard as he could. The car rocked but his hand didn't move.

"Cut it out," someone yelled. Oil glanced at the edge of the crowd. Scuz stared back at him, both hands gripping the rope. Oil moaned a long, low animal sound. He stared blankly for a moment then threw his whole body back. I could see the skin on his hand stretch a little away from the car.

"Arrrrrr," he groaned, then tried again. "Arrrrrrrr," he snarled then threw himself away from the car.

"Stop," cried Scuz but Oil didn't even seem to hear him. Again and again he hurled himself back, but he couldn't break away. His eyes were glazed and his lips moved, swearing silently.

Scuz looked like he was going to jump the barrier.

"Stop right there," yelled Inspector Dawson, pointing at Scuz. He ran up and grasped Oil by the arm. "That's enough now, you're going to hurt yourself."

Oil stared blankly.

"Don't move." Dawson strode to his car and made a call on his radio. Aunty Hepi and I hadn't moved out of the arena. Suddenly Oil hauled himself onto the bonnet, gazed at us, gritted his teeth and threw himself backwards off the bonnet. He fell back, seemed to pause for a moment, then screamed and struck the pavement. There was a patch of his skin still stuck to the car.

"Idiot!" yelled Inspector Dawson as he rushed over to him. He grabbed Oil's arm as he struggled to his feet but Oil pushed him away. There was no skin on his hand, only bloody red flesh.

"No!" Oil cried, breaking into a run and charging to the door of the nearest toilet, a trail of blood dripping onto the tarmac. He shut the door and all we could hear was a splash and a relieved moan.

Inspector Dawson made another call and an ambulance arrived shortly afterwards. The ambulance men wrapped Oil's hand then took him away. I saw Scuz in the crowd leaning towards Oil and saying something before disappearing into the crowd. Vinny reckoned Scuz said "You useless bastard!"

16
Winner Takes All

Aunty Hepi and I gazed at each other for a moment before we started again. She glanced at the skin that remained on the car, shook her head and turned away. It made me feel sick too.

When Matt and Vinny woke up they couldn't get over the amount of skin on the car. "That's half his arm," said Matt.

"I'm surprised it stuck there, it'd be that greasy," cried Vinny.

"What do you think McGreedy'll do about it?" wondered Matt.

Vinny waddled around, pretending to straighten a bow tie. Then he did his best to put on a deep, husky voice. "Ladies and gentlemen, I'd like to offer this superb piece of automotive machinery, and as a special bonus a large section of fresh skin at no extra cost. That's right ladies and gentlemen, no extra cost. It's ideal for those everyday situations where you need a skin graft and haven't got time to get to the . . . " He stopped abruptly. I followed his gaze to where Inspector Dawson was standing with his arms crossed. Mr McGreedy was next to him with a tube of something and some rubber gloves. Matt tried hard not to laugh.

Mr McGreedy chuckled, deep down in his belly. Then he walked across and slapped Vinny on the shoulder. "You'll make a salesman one day kid." He stopped laughing as he put the rubber gloves on and used the tube of solvent to clean the skin and glue off the car. Inspector Dawson frowned and shook his finger at Vinny.

The Tawhitis and Dessy arrived with breakfast just after we started our eight o'clock break. "Where is everyone?" asked Tu, staring around the yard.

"Is it all finished already?" asked Dessy.

"Who won?"

"W . . . what happened?"

Vinny filled everyone in while Aunty Hepi and I tucked into the bacon and egg sandwiches that they'd made. After staying up all night it was more like we were partners than competitors. I glanced up at Dessy while I was eating, she was watching me. Aunty Hepi had obviously seen us last night, 'cos she gave me a big elbow in the ribs and started giggling.

Inspector Dawson waved at us and we went back to the car. My legs and back were sore from standing up for so long. I hoped that we wouldn't have to go for much longer. I tried to relax and concentrate but I kept thinking of Dessy.

The morning dragged on slowly. The gang stood just outside the roped off area.

"Go Dav," called Vinny.

"Go Aunty Hepi," called Tammy at the same time.

Vinny glared at her and she glared back.

"G . . . go D . . . Davin and Aunty Hepi," called Conner. Everyone thought that was great so they cheered for each of us alternately, except for Vinny who refused to cheer for Aunty Hepi. Aunty Hepi couldn't stop laughing, she thought it was the funniest thing she'd ever heard.

I couldn't believe it when Mum chugged up on the tractor halfway through the morning. She came roaring right up to the car yard, the tractor clunking and sending billows of smoke into the sky.

Mr McGreedy went over and talked to her for a minute. I didn't know that Mum knew Mr McGreedy. She seemed surprised, looked around till she spotted me and walked up to the edge of the roped-off area. "Morning Davin, I didn't know you were here."

"Yep," I said. "I've been here for a while."

"So they say, looks like you're doing alright too."

I nodded.

"Fancy that." She shook her head surprised. "Is this what you've been saving up for over the last month?"

"Sort of. I'll tell you when it's finished."

Mum stared at me. "Okay. While I'm here I may as well stay and watch for a while."

"I suppose," I said. "There's not much happening."

Mum shook her head and wandered over to talk to Matt. They seemed to have a lot more to talk about since Matt wasn't living at home any more, and they hardly seemed to argue either.

No matter how tired I was feeling Aunty Hepi didn't seem to change at all. She was still smiling and chatting as if she was at a Sunday picnic. She'd just stopped talking to Mrs Tawhiti when she turned around to me. "You said goodbye to your girlfriend yet?" I shook my head. "You better get on with it then, she's going soon." She grinned. "Give her a nice goodbye and you might see her again next holidays, aye?"

I shuffled my feet. "Yeah, um . . . I'll do that, thanks."

"That's alright boy," she winked. "I can see you two have got the hots for each other." She gave a big happy laugh and turned to talk to another one of her cousins who had dropped by.

Dessy was saying goodbye to everyone else when I got my twelve o'clock break.

"Come back next holidays," said Tu.

"N . . . nice m . . . meeting you."

"Awwww man," cried Tammy, "I hate goodbyes." She gave Dessy a big hug, they both laughed at the other one for looking teary-eyed.

Vinny gave her a sheepish smile. "Great meeting you." She nodded to him and smiled back.

Then I was left in front of Dessy, not really knowing what to say. We both looked each other in the eye for a long moment. Hers were so warm and soft, it was like they could just melt away. "Ummmm," I mumbled, "it's a shame you weren't here longer."

She nodded. "Yeah, I would have liked that." It seemed like there was nothing else to say.

By the time everyone had fluffed around and said what a great summer it had been and how neat it was at the waterhole and laughed about me trying to ride Firebrand, it was time for me to go back to the car. Everyone was still talking so I slipped away quietly.

I watched them walk to where Mrs Tawhiti was waiting to drive Dessy to the bus stop. Suddenly Dessy broke away from the group, glancing around till her eyes rested on me. She slipped away from everyone and in seconds she was right beside me.

She looked like she was going to say something then stopped. Instead she threw her arms around my neck, pulled my face towards her and kissed me on the lips. I was stunned, I could hear everyone cheering and laughing but it didn't mean anything to me. Dessy turned and ran back to the car, giving Tammy a quick hug before she jumped in. The car pulled away and I caught a glimpse of her staring back towards me and waving. I lifted my hand and waved back.

"Bye Dessy," I murmured.

I was still standing there watching the car turn around the corner and disappear when Inspector Dawson tapped me on the shoulder. "Sorry Davin, you've let go of the vehicle, I'll have to disqualify you."

It took a second to register, then I looked at my hand, still in the air. I'd let go of the car to wave at Dessy. I was finished, I'd lost. All that effort and money and I'd lost, and I had nothing to offer to Mum for the old car that I'd destroyed. I put my hand to my side and stumbled away from the car. I could hear people cheering for Aunty Hepi and clapping, and a few people called to me but I couldn't even think. I was broken.

Suddenly Mum and Matt were beside me. They walked me to the office steps and sat me down. I just felt numb, I no longer cared about anything.

"Mum," I said.

"Yeah."

"You know, when the car burnt down," I dropped my eyes, "it was my fault, I ran it back and let the handbrake off. I didn't post the insurance, it was all my fault."

"I know," said Mum.

I stared at her. "You can't."

"I was sure I'd left the handbrake on, then when I was cleaning up I found the hose out and remembered you'd been going to clean the car, it must have been you."

"Why didn't you say?" I couldn't believe it.

"Because you didn't tell me," said Mum. "That's why I didn't tell you I'd found the insurance envelope and posted it a week before."

"You mean it was insured and we didn't have to drive round all summer on the poxy old tractor?"

"Yes we did, I was saving up for that Falcon ute over there. I just need another couple of hundred. That's why I was here this morning to make sure McGreedy didn't sell it first." Mum raised her eyebrows.

"Oh no." I could have cried. "I spent nearly two hundred to enter the Car Challenge. We could have had another car."

Matt had been looking like he was going to wet himself. "Can't you read?" he cried. "Didn't you look at the entry form?"

"Aye?"

"On the form." He pointed to an entry form in his hand. "The person finishing second gets five hundred dollars."

I grabbed it off him and stared at the paragraph he was pointing to. He was right. I was so keen to win the car that I hadn't read the rest. I'd won five hundred dollars, enough to help Mum get the car. I could even keep some of it, I couldn't believe it.

I stood on the stage with Aunty Hepi as Mr McGreedy made his speech. I could see Vinny, Connor, Tu and Tammy in the audience, grinning and pushing each other. Matt and Mum were towards the back, not far from the Falcon ute Mum had been looking at.

"For second spot in the Great Car Challenge I'd like to award Davin Smith a cheque for five hundred dollars. Let's give him a big hand."

I stepped forward, the gang was cheering wildly, Matt whistled from the back and Mum was beaming. Aunty Hepi slapped me on the back. "Good on ya boy." I held the cheque and grinned. I wished Dessy could have seen me standing there.

* * *

Mum, Vinny and I jammed in the front seat of the ute to go home. Matt was going to bring the tractor home later with his motorbike on the tray.

"Y'know," said Vinny. "There's a competition in Wellington where you've gotta hang onto a house. The winner gets to keep the house. I reckon Davin would stand a good chance."

"We've already got a house," said Mum.

"But it never hurts to have a spare one. You never know, it might get burnt down or a flood might carry it away."

"No," I said sleepily. "I'm not entering, I'm going to have a holiday."

"Good idea," Mum agreed. "All your working has left us way behind at home. I've got heaps of jobs for you to do – lawns, gardens, drenching lambs."

"You'll have to clean the new car too," added Vinny, grinning wickedly.

I groaned. "Not even funny."

I was dozing off to sleep when a thought struck

me. “Mum,” I said. “You know how I helped pay for this car?”

“Mmmm,” said Mum.

“So it’s part mine?”

“I suppose it is.” Mum agreed.

“Could you teach me how to drive?”

THE TOM FITZGIBBON AWARD

This award was established in recognition of the outstanding contribution made by the late Tom Fitzgibbon to the growth and status of children's literature in New Zealand.
The award is made annually when merited, at the discretion of the New Zealand Children's Book Foundation, and carries a monetary prize along with an offer of publication by Scholastic New Zealand Limited.

ABOUT THE AUTHOR

Vince Ford was born in Taranaki in 1970 and lives in Karapiro in the Waikato. *2MUCH4U* was written while Vince was completing a writing course at Whitirea Polytech. The story was inspired by an 11-year-old entrepreneur Vince met in Raetihi who had taken up odd jobs like possum hunting to earn some extra money. Vince works as a production manager making agricultural videos, he's also been a teacher aide and a sheep-mustering jackaroo in outback Australia. In his spare time Vince likes to go kayaking, mountain biking and run marathons.

More great books from Scholastic:

GO HORATIO
Pat Quinn

All Amy wants for her birthday is a dog, but she ends up with Horatio – a big, ugly cat with a chewed-up ear. Stubborn old Horatio just isn't interested in learning dog tricks. That is until an unexpected visitor makes a home in Amy's backyard. This hilarious read is the sequel to *Too Chicken*.

HORSE APPLES

Ged Maybury

When Randy and Piho's plan of selling manure to raise funds for their league team takes off, they can't believe their luck. They even land starring roles in a TV commercial that's being made in their country town. But the sweet smell of success turns into a spectacularly stinky ending!

Winner of the Esther Glen Award
Winner of the Premio Andersen Award (Italy)

AGNES THE SHEEP
William Taylor

Agnes is a sheep. A very dirty, smelly sheep with a tendency to butt anyone who gets in her way. So when Belinda and Joe have to find her a new home, they know it isn't going to be easy. How are they to get a massive, mean-tempered sheep across town without disastrous results?